WAR DRUMS OF
EAGLE KING

WAR DRUMS OF
EAGLE KING

KAMARUPA SERIES

P.W. INGTY

PARTRIDGE
A Penguin Random House Company

To order additional copies of this book, contact
Partridge India
000 800 10062 62
orders.india@partridgepublishing.com

www.partridgepublishing.com/india

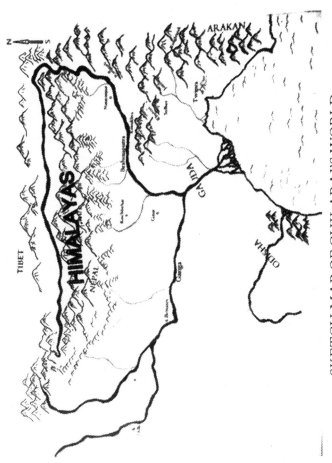

SKETCH MAP OF CHILARAI'S WORLD.

ACKNOWLEDGEMENTS

I am grateful to my family members, relatives and friends, who have always been supportive and have in their own special ways, guided me in my efforts at writing. A special thanks to the Director of Arts & Culture, Shillong and the Archeologist who rendered valuable help during research. My thanks, to the libraries, museums and bookshops, which I had visited to gct information and material for the book. The work would have taken much longer and might have been very different without the internet and Wikipedia.

CHAPTER 1

BLACK EAGLE

The black eagle leaped away from its perch high up on the branches of a gigantic *simul* tree in the forest and glided down silently and gave out a shrill cry. *Eeeiw-kik-kik-kik-kirrr.* The creature on the ground far below did not hear the shrill, high-pitched cry of the black eagle, but the highly sensitive sensory organs located in the jaw and skull of the creature immediately sensed the vibrations in the air waves as the eagle approached, and the serpent's movement suddenly seemed to freeze where it was on the floor of the forest. As the eagle flew down gradually, it positioned itself almost directly above the creature on the ground, then it quickly closed its wings and descended on the creature swiftly like a falling rock, with its feet in position and talons stretched out.

For quite a long time before launching this attack from the sky, the large black eagle had waited patiently, still and unmoving, and only its eyes had moved, focusing on something which was stirring on the ground more than a hundred feet away from where the eagle was perched on the branch of a gigantic *simul* tree in the subtropical forest. The creature on the ground below had moved and stopped; it lay still for some time as if it were watching something, then it moved again in a scissoring movement that could be compared to the letter *S*, expanding and contracting alternately, so common to reptiles of its species. The name given by the locals to this serpent was *daboia*; it was a venomous viper which was found throughout the region. The name of the deadly reptile was appropriate to its nature and ability to lie hidden and lurk in a discreet manner on the floor of the forest. This species of snake was responsible for one of the highest number of snakebite incidents and deaths in the region. Around four feet in length, its head was flattened, triangular, and distinct from the neck. Its snout was blunt, rounded, and raised, and the jaws of the viper had six pairs of fangs. Its eyes were large and flecked with gold and yellow. The stout and rounded body was light yellow on the underside; on the upper side of the body it was dark brown in colour and had three series of dark-brown spots along the whole length of the body. Each spot had a black ring around the outer border, intensified with a rim of white and yellow. The viper moved again in a slow and sluggish manner in the open grassy forest floor studded with scattered bushes. It was quite unaware of the winged predator which was silently watching its progress from its distant perch hidden by the leaves of the tree. The creature below moved again and was for some time in a clear, open patch of the forest floor among rustling dry leaves and short, sparse grass. It was at this vulnerable moment of exposure that the eagle had launched its attack.

Now, at the last moment, when the shadow cast by the eagle had moved rapidly over the immobile snake, it recovered from temporary paralysis and tried to dart away, but it was too late. The reptile on the forest floor was stunned by the force of the impact with the body of the attacking eagle, and the steel-like claws of the eagle caught the head and neck of the lurker in a throttling vice-like grip and twisting it at the same time. The snake's neck bones had dislocated with the impact, and the sharp talons of the eagle had pierced through the tough skin of the neck and soft parts of its skull, reaching to its central nervous system. The *daboia* now struggled weakly as its life ebbed away. The eagle continued to hold its prey on the ground, and at the same time, it attacked the snake a number of times with its sharp, hooked beak, and the struggles of the snake became weaker and weaker. Then, rustling sounds in the forest were heard of someone or something approaching the spot where the eagle was struggling with the snake, someone approaching fast, running through the forest, with feet crashing on dry leaves and twigs, carelessly rushing towards the spot where the eagle had caught its prey. After a while two young boys, one slightly elder and the other his younger sibling of around eleven years, emerged from the far side of the forest clearing and gave surprised exclamations when they saw what the eagle had caught. It was clear that the two boys had been observing the eagle from an unseen location not too far away. The eagle remained crouching, holding its prey down, and waited for the two boys, his young friends, to reach the spot. The two boys were sons of Bisu, leader of the Koch tribe. They had ventured out on a hunting expedition with their eagle. The eagle seemed to have a special bond with the younger of the two brothers, and when they reached the eagle it released the dead serpent and immediately flew up and alighted on the large forked stick which the boy was holding and on which a perch had been fashioned specially for the bird.

Years ago, the eagle had been caught as a chick from its nest by a Koch hunter whose quest for jungle fowl got frustrated, and instead of jungle fowl he had brought down a mother eagle with the arrow released from his bow.

The hunter, who happened to be Bisu's brother, was one of the best hunters of the Koch tribe, and the episode of his hunt for jungle fowl was connected to the cravings of a woman for a dish prepared with tasty chunks of meat of jungle fowl. This woman was Bisu's younger and second wife, Padmawati, who was heavily pregnant with a child. It was at a stage when the woman who was heavy with child longed to taste peculiar kinds of food according to the cravings of her taste buds, which became hyperactive at this stage. There was an age-old belief that the personality of the child to be born would be strongly influenced by what the mother ate during this period of craving for food. Padmawati, at this time, yearned for the flesh of jungle fowl cooked in the simple way that it was done in Kamatapur. At some point in time earlier she had savoured this dish, and now again at this stage of her pregnancy she remembered the dish and wanted to taste it again. She asked Bisu to procure the meat of jungle fowl and to get it prepared for her in that particular fashion with simple ingredients. So Bisu, leader of the Koch tribe, called his brother, who was a reputed hunter, and asked him to procure a jungle fowl within a day and to get it prepared into a dish to the liking of his wife Padmawati. Bisu's brother set out immediately after collecting his bow and arrows and a large cloth bag. He wandered around in the forest, visiting all the usual haunts that were frequented by jungle fowl, but could not spot one in spite of his efforts. It was almost as if all the jungle fowls were hiding from him that day with the knowledge of what he was looking for. Then late in the day and he had still not procured any jungle fowl, and this made him a little irritated. He finally decided to shoot down any big bird resembling a fowl, rather than return empty-handed from the hunt. It was around this time that he spotted a large eagle perched on a tree. The hunter took careful aim and released the arrow from his bow, bringing down the unfortunate eagle with a single arrow; it was a mother eagle, and its nest was located high up on the tree. The hunter had also noticed the eagle's nest high up on the *simul* tree, which he then climbed with some difficulty and was rewarded with the sight of a newly hatched chick in the eagle's nest. The hunter caught the eagle chick, bundled it in his cloth bag, and climbed down from the tree with it. The hunter then quickly returned to his own home, with the still-warm body of the eagle which he had brought down with his arrow. He removed the feathers with his hands; the longer and more elegant feathers of the eagle he kept separately—these he would preserve as souvenirs and for decoration. After de-feathering the eagle the hunter singed the skin of the dead bird over a roaring fire and then cut it into large pieces. The hunter peeled and chopped pieces of onion, small ginger, and garlic and made it into a mixture. He took some black pepper and ground it with pestle and mortar and added the ground pepper to the mixture. The hunter poured some fresh mustard oil in a wide open-mouthed pot and heated the oil. After a while he put the mixture in the heated oil, along with a few bay leaves for flavour, and stirred the contents lightly. When the mixture became a little dry, the pieces of eagle meat were added and cooked slowly till the meat became soft. Salt was added to taste. The aroma of the cooking meat and condiments wafted gently in the air and was carried out by the breeze to the surrounding neighbourhood.

The aroma of the dish caught the attention of the expectant Padmawati, who immediately understood that the hunter was successful in procuring the jungle fowl for her and had also cooked it. She called her maidservant and sent her to bring a piece of the cooked fowl to satisfy her craving. A little while later the maid servant returned from the house of the hunter with a small covered pot containing a well-cooked leg and other meaty pieces of the fowl. The maidservant was under the impression that it was the flesh of a jungle fowl which had been bagged by the hunter, for that was what she had been told. Padmawati ate the leg of the eagle with a little boiled white rice and relished the meal. Her yearning was satisfied, and Bisu's brother the hunter diplomatically kept quiet about the eagle meat. Ignorance was bliss, and Padmawaati lived happily with the belief that she had consumed the delicious flesh of jungle fowl. Later on, in due course of time, she delivered a healthy male baby, who was given the name Sukladhvaj.

On his part, the hunter nurtured the eagle chick which he had taken from the nest till it grew into a fine young eagle, which he trained for hunts. Later on he finally gifted the young eagle to Sukladhvaj and Malladev, sons of his elder brother, Bisu, who were delighted with the rare gift.

CHAPTER 2

ASHRAM IN BENARES

A few years later, the sons of Bisu had grown a little older, a little bigger, and a little stronger. Now their father decided that they needed guidance from a wise teacher, and he was given advice to send them to Benares to the ashram of Guru Brahmananda, where they would be able to receive appropriate guidance and learning. So it was that on a day during the sixteenth century AD, in the well-known ashram run by Guru Brahmananda in the city of Benares, two young men, Malladev and Sukladhvaj, squatted on floor mats along with other young men and listened with rapt attention to their teacher, Brahmananda. The two brothers from the east formed part of a group of young men who were from different places and who had varying backgrounds; the only common thing among them was that they were all under the tutelage of the learned guru Brahmananda.

The two brothers were in the ashram in Benares to fulfil the wish of their father, Bisu, who had hopes of making them into leaders who would sometime in the future be able to guide and lead the Koch community. Bisu had in the course of time taken several wives, and he had a total of eighteen children from these wives, but of all his children, Bisu had a special bond with his two elder sons, namely Malladev and Sukladhvaj. Bisu wanted these two sons to carry on the legacy of his dream for Kamatapur, the Koch kingdom, even after he was gone. The two brothers were, however, still very young and immature, so Bisu decided to send them over to the famous city of Benares to pursue studies in an ashram under the learned sage Brahmananda.

An ashram was in the ancient times a feature of social organization, and this system was said to have been developed during the later Vedic period. It was meant to be a halting place, a temporary place of halting or a stage in life to prepare oneself for further journey. It was a place where the pupils could live with their guru, acquiring knowledge of science, philosophy, scriptures, and logic, practicing self-discipline, and learning to live a life of righteousness. The ashram was also a centre of cultural activity, study of music, yoga, and religious instruction. The residents of an ashram regularly performed spiritual and physical exercises.

Malladev was the elder son of Bisu, and he was born of Hemaprabha of Gaur, the first wife of Bisu. Malladev had sharp features and was built like a young bull; he had wide shoulders and was tall and handsome with dark, tan skin colouring. Sukladhvaj was next to Malladev, and he was born of Padmawati, also of Gaur and the second wife of Bisu. Sukladhvaj in contrast had a broad and strong moon-shaped face with light skin colouring and was lean but strongly built, and he kept his black wavy hair long, hanging down to his shoulders. It somehow gave him a dashing and attractive look. He had taken after his father, Bisu, who had looked almost identical when he was younger. Sukladhvaj also had a sharp mind; his strong point was that he was a good organizer. The two brothers were now pursuing their studies under the learned Brahmananda in Benares. The city was a renowned religious as well as educational hub, to which people came from all over to visit the famous ghats and temples, and scholars went there with the hope of acquiring knowledge that would make them wiser. Bisu was aware of this, and he wanted his two elder sons to benefit from the learning and exposure in that famous city. Maybe one day they would become good leaders of the Koch kingdom which Bisu was trying to establish at Kamatapur. The two brothers, Malladev and Sukladhvaj, were sincere, intelligent, and both were fast learners, but they differed in their personalities. Malladev was fond of wrestling, literature, and cultural activities; he involved himself in discussions and debates with learned persons and participated in plays and dramas in the institute. On the other hand, Sukladhvaj was more inclined towards games and activities which posed a mental and physical challenge, requiring sharpness of wit and quick response. On occasions when the two brothers combined their talents, they formed a very formidable pair.

Brahmananda was quite fond of the two brothers who had been put in his care by the ruler of the eastern kingdom of Kamatapur. They were bright and keen, and Brahmananda was certain that they would make excellent pupils. At the end of the day, Guru Brahmananda asked his pupils a few probing questions to find out whether they had grasped the lessons for the day. After some more discussions on a few important topics, the teacher dismissed them for the day.

'Think about what you have learned today and apply it in different situations. Make an imaginary situation of the consequences of your decisions and actions, and if you have any doubts or questions, you may bring them to me later at any convenient time.'

'Pranam! Guruji.' With palms folded together the pupils thanked Brahmananda as they prepared to leave the hall.

Malladev and Sukladhvaj left the classroom and wandered out into the brick-paved streets of Benares in the early evening. They walked briskly towards one of their favourite sites in the city, the Dashashwamedh Ghat on the banks of the river Ganga. It was one of the oldest ghats in Benares, located close to the Kashi Vishwanath Temple. Legend had it that this ghat was built by Brahma to welcome Shiva and that he had sacrificed ten horses here during one ceremony. The two brothers loved to stroll on the sandy beach of the river at this site in the evening and feel the cool breeze blowing from the river. Sometimes they stopped to watch a group of priests performing Agni puja, or worship of fire, which took place every day in the evening.

The evening was still quite warm, and the two brothers took a quick dip in the river to cool off. Benares was located on the banks of the Ganga; it was a good place, and the brothers lived in Benares for several years in the ashram, and they enjoyed their stay in the city.

Among all his experiences in the ashram of Sage Brahmananda, Sukladhvaj cherished most his exposure to transcendental meditation that was taught in the ashram. There was nothing which could give Sukladhvaj more peace and satisfaction than retreating for a session of transcendental meditation after a normal day filled with activities which had challenged his wits and his mind. It was his habit to sit in an isolated spot on the banks of the river Ganga and slowly relax his body as well as his mind with his eyes closed. His normal breathing naturally slowed down, and the intervals between inhalation and exhalation became longer and longer till it reached a point where it would appear that he was no longer breathing. His mind became completely silent though it was wide awake, and he could remain in this state for a considerable length of time. It was during these sessions of meditation that he could feel his mind becoming detached from the world around him; the mind had transcended beyond the ordinary, and in an inexplicable way it had risen above the mundane existence of the world around him. At these times Sukladhvaj felt tranquil, and a tremendous sense of inner peace and satisfaction filled his mind.

Many times during these sessions of meditation, without his bidding a mysterious vision would appear to him. Sukladhvaj could not understand why the vision appeared, but he guessed that it could be because of some important incident that had taken place during his childhood and which had left a lasting impression on his mind. This vision appeared suddenly when his mind was still and quiet but fully alert. In his vision he was soaring through the sky on wings, like a large bird of prey. The sky was clear and the wind blew against his chest, which was covered by layers of feathers which were smooth and strong, and these feathers deflected the flow of the wind in such a way that he moved up and forward through the air steadily with great speed. During these flights the clarity and strength of his eyesight was greater than at normal times; looking down, he could see far below him the flow of the Ganga River. Some fishing boats were plying on the river, and he could see people crawling around like ants. On the banks of the river he could see temples and people moving in and out of the temples; some people were dipping themselves in the shallow part of the river. As he flew higher and higher the air became chilly, and he saw to the north the snow-capped Himalaya Mountains, and he dipped one wing to change the direction of his flight till he was moving towards the mountains. He continued to fly in this direction for a very long time, and he was surprised that he did not feel weary or faint because of the long flight; his energy and strength seemed to be boundless. He felt so exhilarated by this experience of soaring in the sky above that he gave a joyful shout of exultation, and from deep inside his throat a shrill cry sprang out, ringing through the air: it was the cry of a black eagle. Suddenly the vision disappeared, and Sukladhvaj was brought back to reality with a shock. His mind cleared, and he was once again squatting on the banks of the Ganga River in Benares.

CHAPTER 3

THE SULTAN'S EXPEDITIONS

In those years in the early part of the sixteenth century, when the Koch community was being shaped into a nation under Bisu's guidance, a number of changes were taking place. Some of these changes went side by side with fierce struggles between different nations and communities that were competing with each other for resources and regional domination. To the east of the Koch-inhabited areas lay regions that were largely under the rule of Ahoms, who were a rising power in the east, and to the south of the Koch areas was Gauda, which at this time was under Muslim rulers. There were frequent conflicts between the Muslims and the Ahoms, which was mainly due to the quest of the Muslim rulers of Gauda for new territories that were rich in forests, farmland, water, elephants, gold, precious stones, and other valuable resources. The Koches warily watched the conflicts between the Ahoms and Muslim armies of Gauda, and they learnt from these turmoils: they saw the use of elephants in warfare, they watched in wonder as they saw them firing volleys from small cannons, and they saw the use of boats in naval warfare. They also knew that sooner or later they could also be drawn into the conflicts. The Koches under Bisu at this time were merely a small rising power compared to the Ahoms, who were powerful enough to take on the armies of the Muslim rulers of Gauda. The great sultan of Gauda ruled over a vast territory stretching southwards up to the shores of the Bay of Bengal, but he was keen to expand his territories to the north and east, which were known to be rich in elephants and ivory, among other things, and rumoured to have a small but endless source of gold, precious stones, and valuable wood. This greatly attracted the sultan of Gauda, who sent expeditions into the eastern region, but it also brought the sultan of Gauda into conflict with the Ahoms.

In 1529 the sultan of Gauda sent an expedition into the north-eastern region; the expedition was headed by a man known as Bit Malik. The expedition moved on fifty large boats and ships; they were equipped with muskets and cannons, in addition to the usual daggers, axes, swords, shields, spears, and bows and arrows. Bit Malik stood at the prow of his ship as it moved up the great river; the breeze from the river blew on his face, and his cotton tunic pressed against his body as he stood there, with the flag of the sultan of Gauda fluttering in the breeze on a bamboo pole which stretched above him. He felt honoured to be placed in charge of this expedition into the mysterious region which had earlier been known as Kamarupa, but over many years, with changes of ruling dynasties and communities, the name Kamarupa had fallen out of use. Bit Malik was curious to know more about this ancient land and its people.

As the expedition moved up the Brahmaputra River, the members of the expedition from Gauda could see the beautiful countryside on either side of the river. Many times they saw herds of elephants frolicking on the banks of the river; once or twice they spotted a few of the great one-horned rhinoceros grazing on the grasslands and looking like giant dung beetles. Herds of sambar and other deer could be seen, and birds, like pelicans and hornbills, flew overhead and nested on the large trees which grew on the riverside. The countryside was rich with all kinds of wildlife.

The movement of the fleet of boats under the command of Bit Malik was observed and keenly watched by the Ahom commander of the area, known as Barpatra Gohain. He stood with some of his colleagues and troops on a high ridge of a range of hills overlooking the Brahmaputra River and saw the ships and boats plying upriver. The Ahom commander continued to monitor the progress of the invaders discreetly, with the use of scouts who watched from the forested hills flanking the river, and others lay hidden in the tall grass and bushes on the sandy banks of the river. The strategy of the Ahoms was to ambush the invaders from Gauda as and when they alighted from their boats. Every twist and turn of the river on this stretch was known to the Ahoms; they knew where the vessels of the invading force would face problems and where they would have to slow down because of sandbars or rocks and rapids. In some places the boatmen would have to use long bamboo poles to push the boats through shallow water flowing over sandy riverbed, and the speed of their boats would be greatly reduced. Barpatra Gohain had also made an attempt to assess approximately where the vessels would have to stop and make a landing. He sent one team of scouts to watch and report back on the progress of the boats, and with the rest of his troops the Ahom commander prepared to attack the expedition led by Bit Malik as and when the boats made a landing on the banks of the Brahmaputra.

Late in the afternoon one day, Bit Malik spotted a habitation not very far from the banks of the river. The riverbank at this site was also very convenient for landing the ships and boats, and it seemed the right place to land and replenish their supplies of food and water before moving further. Bit Malik spoke to the master of the ship, who in turn gave the signal for making a landing of the fleet of ships and boats. They had been traveling on the river for a number of days and weeks; the men were weary of the journey, and they now disembarked from the boats to stretch their legs on land to get some relief. Bit Malik's troops started disembarking from the boats, and some of the troops started offloading the guns and cannons from the vessels.

This was a great opportunity for the waiting Ahoms, and the Ahom Barpatra Gohain immediately took advantage of this vulnerable moment and attacked

Bit Malik's army before they were even in a position to use their guns and cannons. The surprised Gauda troops rallied to respond to the sudden attack, but they were already at a disadvantage and could not put up an effective resistance. Bit Malik's troops were routed in the fight, and they finally fled back to their vessels, leaving behind their cannons and guns, which fell into the hands of the Ahoms. Bit Malik fought bravely, but he was separated from the rest of his troops during the desperate fighting, and then unfortunately he was surrounded by Ahom fighters, who prevented him from escaping with the rest of his troops. He was captured by the Ahoms and executed. After this misadventure of the Bit Malik–led expedition from Gauda, there were no fresh incursions into this frontier region for a few years.

The sultan of Gauda nursed the wounds inflicted on his prestige by the disaster of the Bit Malik expedition for some years, and then he sent another expedition under an experienced Afghan general named Turbak Khan. Turbak was given command over a large army comprising both land and naval forces, and with this impressive and powerful army he invaded the territories under Ahom influence. The forces led by Turbak Khan were well equipped with sufficient rations and armaments; their soldiers were well trained and seemed unbeatable as they moved steadily on the north bank of the Brahmaputra towards the core of the Ahom-held territories. The Ahom king Suklenmung, with his army, confronted Turbak Khan's forces at Singri. There was a fierce battle at Singri in which Suklenmung was wounded and the expeditionary force from Gauda got the upper hand. The wounded Suklenmung retreated to Sala with his army, and they were pursued by the seasoned Turbak Khan, who handed the retreating Ahoms another defeat at Sala. This forced the Ahoms to retreat across the Brahmaputra to the south bank of the river, where they adopted a different tactic.

Turbak Khan, having tasted victory in the initial skirmishes with the Ahoms, felt elated and full of confidence; now he was sure that he would succeed in his mission of taming this region, and he lost no time in pursuing after the retreating Ahoms by crossing over to the south bank of the river Brahmaputra.

The Ahoms made a swift change of tactics after crossing over to the south bank of the Brahmaputra. A wing of the Ahom army was secretly sent in boats to sail down the Brahmaputra River till they reached behind the forces from Gauda. Then this Ahom force positioned itself in such a way as to cut off all supply and communication lines of Turbak Khan's army with their homeland and headquarters in Gauda. The indomitable Turbak Khan, however, decided to press on with his expedition in spite of this setback and also to depend upon locally available resources. Turbak Khan's forces soon reached the Dikrai River, where they found that the Ahoms had positioned themselves on the other bank of the river under Ahom general Tonkham, an experienced fighter. By this time Suklenmung, the Ahom king, had expired and his son Suhungmung had taken his place. Suhungmung had entrusted Ahom general Tonkham with the task of driving back the Muslim invasion. At this point in time, Turbak Khan's army was already running low on rations, and there were no reinforcements or fresh supplies coming from Gauda. As a consequence of which the troops under Turbak Khan were in no position to take on the strongly entrenched Ahoms on the other bank of the Dikrai River, so they waited and watched. The Ahoms were now in their own element, as they knew the region and the lay of the land much better than Turbak Khan's army, and they now launched a series of guerrilla attacks on the army of Turbak Khan, harassing them endlessly. These guerrilla attacks inflicted serious damage to the Muslim forces and affected their morale adversely. Turbak Khan tried to manoeuvre to a better position, but he was unable to do so in spite of his best efforts, and his army suffered many setbacks. When Turbak's army had been bled and weakened, the main army of the Ahoms moved against them from strong positions, even as they tried to manoeuvre and avoid full-pitched battles. The Ahoms were now successful in turning the tide of the battle against Turbak's army in a number of major engagements, and finally in the battle near the Bharali River, the Ahom general Tonkham completely routed Turbak Khan's forces. In the pitched battle that was fought on the banks of the Bharali River, Turbak Khan died fighting the Ahoms, and when the Muslim soldiers saw that their commander was vanquished, they gave up the fight and fled towards Gauda, hotly pursued by the Ahoms. These fleeing troops were pursued by the Ahoms up to a point beyond the Karotiya River in the northern part of present-day Bangladesh. Many of Turbak Khan's troops were also captured, and the Ahoms settled these captured Muslim soldiers in a particular place. These Muslim soldiers who were captured and settled at that place were called Garias by the local inhabitants, Garias meaning 'people who were originally from Gaur'. The Garias thus became the first significant Muslim community in the north-eastern region. Later on some of them were engaged as soldiers; others became very good cultivators and artisans who were famed for their brass work.

CHAPTER 4

BISU

As the victorious soldiers under Ahom general Tonkham returned from chasing after the fleeing soldiers of the slain Turbak Khan to a point beyond the Karotiya River and moved back to the east, they had to pass through territories under Koch influence. One fine morning, Tonkham spotted a large contingent of Koch troops led by Bisu near the Teesta River; the Koch troops appeared to be in battle formation yet made no aggressive move against the Ahoms. Bisu and several of his commanders, mounted on horses, watched the Ahoms warily from the gentle slopes of a small hillock, and the Ahoms under Tonkham looked back at the Koches, a little confused about the intentions of Bisu and his troops. Bisu had taken care to be positioned at a strategic point from where he could attack effectively or retreat safely in case the Ahoms became hostile. Tonkham wondered whether the Koches had joined forces with the Muslims, in which case it would be a folly to just pass them by and continue. Tonkham issued orders to one of his commanders, and at a signal from him, a wing of the Ahom army turned towards the Koches and moved rapidly to engage them. Bisu allowed them to come closer, then he signalled to the flag bearers with a slight nod of his head, and at his signal one of the flag bearers raised a single white peace flag and a small group of four unarmed Koch horsemen rode slowly towards the Ahoms. On seeing this the Ahom commander raised his hand, and the Ahom troops slowly came to a halt and waited with curiosity for the small group of approaching Koches. On reaching the Ahom commander the Koches stopped, and one of them who knew the Ahom language spoke to the Ahom *saikia*.

'We bear greetings from our leader, Bisu. The Koches have no enmity with the Ahoms, and we have great respect for Suhungmung, ruler of the Ahoms. Our leader, Bisu, sends congratulations to Ahom general Tonkham for his victory against the Muslims, and he also invites the general for a feast to celebrate the occasion and to talk terms of friendship.'

The Ahom *saikia* dispatched one of his men to convey the message to Ahom general Tonkham. The mounted soldier turned his horse around and rode quickly to the place where Tonkham waited with the rest of the army. The message was relayed to General Tonkham, who gave a grunt of relief and satisfaction. The Ahoms were still far from their headquarters, and Tonkham felt that it was a good idea to spare a little time for some rest and merriment.

'Tell them that I accept the invitation.'

In the feast organized by Bisu for the Ahom general, a warm relationship was soon established between the Koches and the Ahoms. The food was delicious, and the performance of the Koch dancers was delightfully entertaining, and everybody had a marvellous time.

After the feast, Tonkham invited the Koch leader to the court of the Ahom king, to be present during the annual gathering of all nobles and rulers of states and kingdoms that had come under the influence of the Ahoms. The Koch leader accepted the invitation.

Later on, Bisu attended the gathering in the Ahom king's capital and offered rich gifts and tribute to Suhungmung. The Ahom king was very pleased with the conduct of the Koch leader, and on the advice of Tonkham, the newly conquered territories of Patladoh, Ghoraghat, Eghara-Sendur, Fariabad, and Sherpur in the west were placed under the administration of the Koch leader Bisu. This arrangement worked for some time, but Bisu was too ambitious and independent to remain for too long as a subordinate ruler under the Ahoms. He soon started making moves for more autonomy.

At a time when Malladev and Sukladhvaj were still undergoing training and studies in Sage Brahmananda's ashram in Benares, their father, Bisu, was occupied with mobilizing his community and kingdom in Kamatapur, the most important centre of the Koch kingdom in those days. Bisu was recognized as leader of the Koches. The Koches were of mixed Mongoloid stock, and they lived in a scattered manner, mostly in the region lying between that part of the river Ganga and the river Brahmaputra in the northern areas of Bengal and western parts of Kamarupa. They were very closely allied to the Meches, Garos, and other tribes of the region. The Koch language was in fact very similar to that of the Garos, and even their customs were akin in those days. Like the Garos, the Koches were also accustomed in those days to using large earrings and other devices at a very young age, and this practice drew out the length of their ears, artificially giving the ears a very long span.

Bisu was a clever and charismatic leader, and he started a systematic organization of the Koch community. In his endeavour to establish a kingdom, Bisu was also able to unite under his leadership members of other tribes who lived in the region in small scattered groups. In this way people from Mech, Bodo, Tephu, Garo, and other tribes came to join the Koches under Bisu. They came together because in Bisu they recognized a leader who was capable of giving them security and of leading them to greater prosperity. He appointed twelve ministers, called *karjis*, to assist him in governing the Koch kingdom. Each of the ministers represented one of the twelve Koch clans. The twelve Koch clans were the Panbar, Phedela, Phedphedo, Barihana, Kathia, Gaubar, Megha, Baisagu, Jagai, Gurikata, Jugbar, and Dakharu clans. These twelve clans had united under Bisu to form the Koch nation. The far-sighted Bisu then conducted a census of the population and made an estimate of the number of able-bodied men in the kingdom. The conduct of a census was one of the first of its kind in the region, and the carrying out of this exercise gave him the information and a tool by which he was able to make a fairly accurate assessment of the potential military strength of the Koch community.

Bisu established a structured society in which administrative functions as well as military functions were combined in the same authority. In this structure, each able-bodied man was called a *paik*, and 20 *paiks* were under the command of a *thakuria*, 100 *paiks* came under the command of a *saikia*, 1,000 *paiks* were under the command of a *hazari*, 3,000 *paiks* were under the command of the *omra*, and 66,000 *paiks* were under the command of a *nawab*. With this united and structured force at his command, Bisu was now prepared to take on his powerful neighbours the *bhuyans*.

The *bhuyans* were an interesting class of landlords and chiefs. Historically, they were not associated with any particular community or tribe but were originally a class of officers who had been entrusted with the assessment of land revenue during the rule of the Pala dynasty in ancient Kamarupa.

The *gomatha* of Ouguri was one of the *bhuyans* whose landholdings lay adjacent to the territories controlled by the Koches. The *gomatha*'s grandfather had in years gone by served the Pala king of Kamarupa as a humble revenue officer, whose duty was to assess the revenue which could be collected from the villages that had been placed under his charge. The land was fertile and yielded good crops of paddy and acres of golden mustard; many productive coconut trees and other fruit trees also grew there. There were plenty of clear, flowing streams and deep ponds rich with fish and other aquatic life. The revenue officer had then assessed the value of the produce in such a way that every year he could easily collect and submit a handsome amount to the Pala ruler of Kamarupa. He also earned a substantial commission from the revenue collected from the villages under his charge. Life was good for the *gomatha*'s grandfather, and as the years passed by he noticed that the hold of the Pala ruler over the revenue collectors was becoming weaker than before. Every *bhuyan*, including the grandfather of the Ouguri *gomatha*, now took opportunity of this changing situation to enrich himself and become more independent by reporting less and less revenue from their respective charges. Gradually each *bhuyan* slowly became the lord of his own territory, and some of them started maintaining small armies to establish their authority over their respective jurisdictions. By the time the *gomatha*'s grandfather passed away, he had amassed sufficient wealth in land and soldiers to enable his descendants to live like mini potentates.

The *bhuyans* had no affinity to any particular ethnic group, religion, or caste, and in the course of time as the power of the Palas dissipated, this class of revenue officers took full opportunity of the weakening and decline of their erstwhile masters and became transformed into powerful landlords and warrior chiefs.

By and by as ancient Kamarupa disintegrated into smaller kingdoms and territories ruled by local satraps, the *bhuyans* began to exercise more political influence and became a new class of rulers. Some of these *bhuyans* were quite oppressive and harassed the poorer sections of people who lived within their holdings, as a result of which the oppressed people revolted from time to time.

The *bhuyans* also had control over the markets in their territories and collected fees and taxes from traders and all people who came to these markets for transaction and barter of goods, and in this process some people faced harassment, which was deeply resented. Bisu now took advantage of the situation and campaigned against the *bhuyans* surrounding the Koch territories. His strategy was to unite various tribal groups, such as the Mech, Bodo, Koch Garo, Tephu, and others, against the oppressive *bhuyans* and to take on the *bhuyans* one by one. Bisu first proceeded against the nearest one, who happened to be the *bhuyan* of Ouguri. On one fine day, the *gomatha* of Ouguri was shocked to see a host of armed Koch *paiks*, tribesmen, and clansmen invading his territory. He at once mobilized his armed men to resist the invaders but was defeated after a brief fierce struggle. Then the defeated *bhuyan* of Ouguri surrendered, and with his armed men he pledged support to the forces of the Koch leader Bisu. Next Bisu moved against the *bhuyan* of Jhargaon, who was similarly routed in a battle. The defeated *bhuyan* of Jhargaon also surrendered and joined Bisu's army with his own armed men. In this way, gradually the forces under Bisu began to swell and grow in size as well as strength. Then Bisu took the combined forces and moved against the *bhuyan* of Karnapur. The prosperous township of Karnapur was ruled by a shrewd *bhuyan* by the name of Chham. The *gomatha* of Karnapur had already heard about the success of Bisu against the *bhuyans* of Ouguri and Jhargaon. He therefore immediately took steps to protect his holdings and the township against the approaching Koch forces; he convened a meeting of his council forthwith. Chham summoned his *hazarikas* for an emergency meeting, and the *hazarikas*, who had been expecting the call, hurried to the venue of the meeting as soon as they received information. Chham greeted them, and initiating the meeting, he enquired about the defensive structures of the township and their condition; he also asked about the alertness of the *paiks* who were guarding the entries into Karnapur. The *hazarikas* informed Chham that all defensive structures were in position and being manned and checked by *paiks* daily. They also informed that all the *saikias* and *thakurias* were regularly monitoring the alertness of the guards.

For the next one hour or so, the discussion of the council focused on their defensive strategy, and a review was made of the supply of rations for the troops and availability of food and other commodities for the townsfolk. After reviewing their preparedness, Chham felt a little less anxious about the situation.

A few days later, Bisu's troops arrived at the boundary of Karnapur, but their further progress was impeded by the defensive structures, which pierced and wounded some of the men and horses in the front, and the troops of Karnapur also showered arrows on the invaders. The Koches attacked the defenders but were repelled by Chham's soldiers.

This was a convincing show of strength, and the Koches became aware that the defence of the township was strong and the troops well dug in. Bisu decided not to waste more valuable soldiers in an all-out frontal attack on Karnapur at this stage, and he waited and watched patiently for a chance to take the defenders by surprise. This opportunity came soon enough with the ripening of grains in the vast paddy fields surrounding Karnapur. The fragrance of the ripening grains of new paddy was noticeable in the warm dry breeze which blew over the green fields of paddy stalks heavy with grains. Bisu then quickly took advantage of the approach of the festive harvest season. There was an unspoken temporary halt to hostilities during this period in which the harvesting of crops took place without interference.

A few weeks later, the harvesting of crops was just over, and the granaries were full with the paddy harvest of the season. The weather was bright and sunny, but it was no longer hot or humid; temperatures were just right for merrymaking and outdoor picnics. There was a light mood in the air, and this was the time when the Kamrupans observed a festival known as Bhogali Bihu, and it was a time for feasting and merriment at the end of harvest. Even though the atmosphere had become tense again as the siege of Karnapur by the Koches had once more been put in place, even this could not suppress the spirit of the common people, who started preparations for the ensuing festival of Bhogali Bihu. The quick-thinking Bisu immediately seized the opportunity and sent several baskets of *pithas* and coconut sweets to the *bhuyan* of Karnapur with Bihu greetings. Chham accepted the gifts and reciprocated by sending choice sweetmeats and the famous Karnapur ladoos. He also conveyed a message requesting for peaceful celebrations of the festival of Bhogali Bihu, and Bisu appeared to respond positively to this message from Chham. In this slightly relaxed environment, there was some easing of the tension between the two opposing camps. It was mid January and the next day was the day of the festival. Everyone was excited on this day, known as Uruka, particularly the young people, who gathered together and went outdoors to spots near the river, carrying with them various articles, musical instruments, and food items. On reaching the selected spots they built makeshift huts, and for building material they used bamboo, twigs, and branches and hay from dry paddy fields. These temporary structures were known as *meji*, and it was around these structures that the young people then lit bonfires and spent the entire Uruka night playing games, feasting, dancing, and singing, and by the time the merriment stopped it would be long past midnight. Most of the men who were members of the Karnapur *bhuyan*'s army were from the outlying villages and towns of the territory which was under the control of the *bhuyan*, and they were now influenced by the festive atmosphere and longed to visit their near and dear ones during the festival, so they sought permission from the *bhuyan* to make a brief visit to their homes to take part in the festivities. The friendly exchange of Bihu gifts between Bisu and the *bhuyan* of Karnapur had eased tensions, and Chham had lowered the strict vigil at the boundary of the township to some extent. Chham felt a little relaxed, and when he received the request from his men for taking part in the festivities, he felt that no harm would come if he allowed some of his men to disperse to their villages and homes for a short time. This, however, turned out to be a great folly and that slip of guard, for which Bisu had been waiting patiently.

As soon as Chham took the decision and allowed some of his men to leave for their villages, Bisu immediately mobilized a particular contingent of Koch soldiers who had been resting in a hiding place away from people's sight during these days. Deprived of the usual festive activities, they were restless for some action, and around midnight following Uruka, these Koch troops were awakened and made battle ready. They were rested, alert, and ready for action.

A little before the break of dawn, Koch troops silently invaded the township of Karnapur and dismantled the defensive structures at some key points to enable the army to enter the township with ease. Flaming torches were lit once they had breached the defensive structures, and with these flaming torches the Koch set fire to property, and simultaneously, with blood-curdling war cries, they fell on the few unsuspecting troops and sleeping citizens of Karnapur, who woke up to the horror of the treacherous attack. There was a fierce struggle as the troops and citizens of Karnapur tried to rally to the defence of the town, and the fighting lasted for a few hours, but by dawn Karnapur had fallen to the Koch forces. Chham was captured and subsequently executed along with some of his loyal followers. Subsequent to the fall of Karnapur, Bisu's attentions turned to the *bhuyans* of Phulaguri, Bijni, and Pandunath, which were subdued by his troops one by one, and afterwards these *bhuyans* also joined forces with Bisu.

The remaining *bhuyans* could not withstand the combined might of the Koches and their subsequently acquired additional forces from the *bhuyans* who had joined with them, and within a period of around twelve years Bisu was able to get the submission of all the *bhuyans* on the north bank of the Brahmaputra up to Barnadi in the east. Most of the defeated *bhuyans* accepted Bisu as their overlord and joined their forces with the Koch, thereby increasing the size and power of the Koch kingdom to a greater extent. As a consequence the Koch kingdom was established on the north bank of Brahmaputra River, which extended over a territory ranging between the Karotiya River to the west and the Barnadi River to the east. It became a power to be reckoned with. Bisu also imported many Brahmans from Kanauj, Benares, and other centres of learning to his capital, and he shifted the capital of the Koch kingdom to Kochbehar, where he built a fine city.

The Brahmans of the region were quick to recognize Bisu's abilities and achievement; they therefore sought to influence him with their theories and ideas. They made up a story that Bisu's tribesmen were Kshatriyas who had thrown away their sacred threads when they were fleeing from a furious Parsuram, the son of the Brahman ascetic Jamadagni, who had been murdered brutally by the sons of the Kshatriya king Kartavirya. The Brahmans then declared Bisu to be none other than the son of the god Shiva, who had taken the form of Bisu's humble father, Hariya, and had intercourse with Hariya's wife, Hira.

Following this Brahmanization, Bisu the tribal assumed the name of Biswa Singha, and many of his followers discarded their old tribal designation and called themselves *rajbansis*. Biswa Singha became a great patron of Hinduism, worshipping Shiva and Durga and offering gifts to priests, to astrologers, and to the disciples of Vishnu.

Bisu then embarked on the project of reconstructing the Kamakhya Temple, which had earlier been damaged by Muslim forces under Turbak Khan. After reconstructing the Kamakhya Temple beautifully, Bisu decided that it was time for him to retire from the active life of ruler of the Koch kingdom. He was fifty-four years old, and as he was not in the best of health; he had found it more and more difficult every passing day to cope with the demanding work of leading the

Koch nation. He finally took a decision to abdicate from kingship in favour of his son Malladev. He therefore convened the highest council of *karjis* and declared before them his decision to abdicate in favour of his eldest son, Malladev. He also urged upon the *karjis* to pledge their support to Malladev to succeed him as king of the Koch Kingdom. After retiring, Bisu retreated to the mountains in the foothills of the Himalayas to live out his remaining days in quiet and peace. Bisu had become weary of the active life which he had led as chief of the Koch kingdom; only after retirement to the forested mountains, Bisu found the surroundings conducive to meditation and spiritual pursuits. He lived for a little longer before finally passing away. Around this time Malladev and Sukladhvaj were still pursuing their studies in Benares under sage Brahmananda.

CHAPTER 5

NARA SINGHA

There was one young man who deeply resented the decision taken by Bisu to abdicate in favour of Malladev before retiring to the mountains. This young man was Nara Singha, a nephew of Bisu who had become quite close to Bisu during the long absence of Malladev and Sukladhvaj, who were away and undergoing training in the ashram at Benares under Sage Brahmananda. The ambitious young man had shared many experiences with his uncle Bisu during the building up of the Koch kingdom; he was quite capable and also elder to his cousin Malladev, and this had led him to imagine that he could take over the leadership of the Koch kingdom after Bisu. It was unfortunate for him that Bisu thought otherwise. The fact was that Nara Singha was a scholarly person, fond of religious discourses and rituals, which had also been observed by Bisu, and though Nara Singha had accompanied Bisu on many campaigns and also shared so many experiences with him, Bisu had always felt that Nara Singha would never make the strong leader which the Koch kingdom needed at this time. Moreover, Malladev not only had all the personal qualities of head and heart that were required for a strong leader, he was also Bisu's own elder son.

Nara Singha therefore became very bitter when he heard that Malladev had been named as Bisu's successor, and he fumed with anger and resentment. Nara Singha expressed his anger and frustration at being bypassed to his own mother. He confided in his mother that all these years, he was under the impression that his uncle Bisu was grooming him to take over the leadership of the Koch kingdom after him, and now he felt betrayed by his uncle's decision to bypass him and name his cousin Malladev as his successor. Nara Singha felt that it was he who had struggled along with Bisu to build up the Koch kingdom and gathered the experience required to be the leader of the Koches. In his own opinion, Nara Singha felt that he rightfully deserved to be the leader with all the experience he had gathered and which he felt Malladev lacked as he had been away in the ashram of Sage Brahmananda in Benares, doing God knows what.

Nara Singha's mother told him to place his claim for leadership before the Koch *karjis* and they would take their decision on his claim. Nara Singha took his grievance to the council of the twelve *karjis* and asked them to take a decision on who should lead the Koch nation. The Koch *karjis*, who had been appointed by Bisu, respected the last wishes of their erstwhile leader, Bisu, and were therefore not inclined to support the claim made by Nara Singha. Before leaving for the high mountains of the Himalayas on retirement, Bisu had very clearly declared in the council of *karjis* that Malladev should be his successor, and the *karjis* had taken a pledge to support Malladev. The bitterly disappointed Nara Singha now rebelled and declared himself to be the rightful successor to the throne of the Koch kingdom, against the will of the *karjis*.

The *karjis* discreetly and swiftly sent messengers to Benares to inform Malladev and Sukladhvaj about the latest turn of events in Kochbehar and also about their rebellious cousin, Nara Singha.

The messengers travelled swiftly from Kochbehar to Benares and delivered the message to the two brothers. On receiving the news, Malladev and Sukladhvaj decided to return to Kochbehar immediately. The two brothers then called upon Guru Brahmananda and explained the situation to him. Guru Brahmananda listened to them calmly, and after analyzing the information he urged them to proceed with caution to Kochbehar on their mission with his blessings. The two brothers expressed their gratefulness to the guru for his understanding and wise guidance during all these years. Then they immediately made their preparations and left for Kochbehar swiftly.

A few days later, when they were still on their way to Kochbehar, they suddenly saw at some distance a great host of soldiers gathered together, and they seemed to be waiting for something. Being unsure about the identity of the gathered host of troops, the travellers stopped and hid themselves in the jungle surrounding the road, and from a concealed place they carefully examined the gathered army, and after a while Sukladhvaj exclaimed quietly, 'They are Koch soldiers, I recognize them by their clothes and the banners carried by the standard bearers.'

Malladev agreed with Sukladhvaj. 'That's right, I recognize those colours, let us send one of the messengers to find out why they have gathered here.'

The lone messenger sent by Malladev proceeded towards the gathered host, and when they saw him approaching, the commander of the troops barked out an order and immediately a small group of soldiers mounted horses and rode towards him. They met him and took him to the commander. There was a longish conversation, after which the messenger was offered a horse, on which he rode back along the road to the spot where the others were waiting in hiding and full of anxiety. On reaching them he informed that the soldiers claimed to be supporters of Malladev and that they were waiting to escort him to Kochbehar. One senior *karji* was also accompanying the soldiers to receive Malladev and his brother. From that point of the journey, the brothers were escorted by this great host of soldiers to their destination.

Two days later, Malladev and Sukladhvaj entered Kochbehar triumphantly. Nara Singha came to know in advance about the progress of Malladev towards Kochbehar, and finding no support from the *karjis*, he, along with his family and a few followers, fled towards the mountains to the north and west of Kochbehar a few days before the two brothers arrived. When Nara Singha arrived at the foothills of the Himalayas, he and his followers were received and given shelter and protection by the Morang raja. The Morang raja was the leader of the Tephus, a community who had settled in the foothills of the Himalayas, on the southern fringes of Nepal, Sikkim, and Bhutan.

In Kochbehar, Malladev ascended to the throne of the Koch kingdom, and he also appointed his brother Sukladhvaj as the commander-in-chief of the Koch army. The first mission given by Malladev to the commander-in-chief of his army was to pursue and capture the rebellious Nara Singha.

The Koch troops led by Sukladhvaj pursued Nara Singha and proceeded towards the foothills of the Himalayas, and as they reached the foothills they were attacked by the Tephus, led by the Morang raja. However, the Tephus were easily subdued by the Koch troops, and their chief was captured and brought before Malladev. The Morang chief surrendered and became a vassal of the Koch ruler.

When Nara Singha saw that the Morang raja had surrendered, he fled from there to Nepal, and later on he went further to Kashmir.

After neutralizing Nara Singha, a ceremony was held at Kochbehar where Malladev formally assumed the title Nar Narayan. Sukladhvaj, who became the commander-in-chief of the Koch forces, was bestowed the title Sangram Singha.

CHAPTER 6

A HIGHWAY TO THE EAST

At the time when the Koch nation was on the rise, the Ahom king Suhungmung ruled over the territories to the east of the Koch-inhabited areas, and during his time relations with the Koches were friendly enough. On the behest of General Tonkham, who had become quite friendly with Bisu, the Koch leader agreed to make a visit to the Ahom king. He went to Suhungmung and presented gifts to the Ahom king. Bisu was treated well, and when he returned to Kamatapur, he was escorted by a unit of Ahom guards of honour. However, deep inside his mind, Bisu was not satisfied; he was ambitious, and it was not in his makeup to remain subordinate to the Ahoms.

Hidden beneath the horizon of friendship between the Ahoms and the Koch were dark clouds of tension, and the situation became more strained because of a son of Suhungmung by the name of Suklen. This prince was quite a spoilt young man; he was disobedient and not loyal to his father. In fact, at one point in time,

Suhungmung feared that he could face incitement to rebellion from Suklen, and he had immediately summoned his queen, Suklen's mother, and asked her to take an oath in the customary tradition and practice of the Ahoms by dipping her right hand in water and by swearing that at all times and under any circumstances she and her son, Suklen, would remain loyal to Suhungmung. Suklen, however, thought nothing of such a symbolic act but kept silent and plotted to get rid of the old king.

He soon got an opportunity to hit the Ahom king through one of Suhungmung's personal attendants by the name of Ratimon. Ratimon was a Kachari who belonged to one of the noble families of the Kachari kingdom, which had been enslaved when the Kacharis were brought under the Ahom rule. Ratimon had ambition, and he always felt that one day he would become something more than a mere slave of the Ahom king, and this urge led him to look for opportunities and take all kinds of risks. This trait of Ratimon was noted by the treacherous Suklen, who then befriended Ratimon and quietly promised him a better position in life with suitable rewards when he became the Ahom king after Suhungmung.

Suklen procured a very sharp dagger and coated it with poison; this was given to Ratimon to perform the tragic deed. Ratimon was a regular visitor to the king's private rooms in order to perform various personal duties for Suhungmung, and therefore the palace guards did not have a reason to suspect treachery from him. One fateful night, Ratimon stealthily entered Suhungmung's bedroom long after the king had retired to bed and stabbed Suhungmung, who cried out aloud in pain before succumbing to the fatal injury. It was a tragic end for a bold, enterprising, and resourceful ruler who had ruled brilliantly for forty-two years. A palace guard who was close by heard the cry and rushed towards the bedroom and confronted Ratimon, who was trying to rush away. The palace guard looked into the king's chamber and saw him lying in a pool of blood; he rushed out again and shouted at Ratimon to stop running. The fugitive started running even faster, then the palace guard threw his spear at the fleeing murderer. The spear flew through the air and struck Ratimon's back between the shoulder blades, and he fell to the ground fatally wounded.

After the assassination of Suhungmung, his son, the treacherous Suklenmung, became the ruler of the Ahom kingdom.

On the south bank of the Brahmaputra was a small fort, the Sola Fort. This fort was occupied by a small contingent of Koch soldiers who represented the authority of the Koch kingdom, and the Ahoms looked on this with some contempt and disfavour. One day, the Ahom king Suklenmung sent an officer, Bar Sandikai, to drive the Koch soldiers out of the Sola Fort. Bar Sandikai proceeded to Sola Fort and besieged it; he asked for an urgent meeting with the *thakuria* in charge of the Koch soldiers and told him to leave the fort with all his men.

'Thakuria! This is Ahom territory, you are to leave this place and cross over to the other side of the Brahmaputra with your *paiks*. I will be returning to Sola Fort tomorrow morning with my soldiers to set up our camp. We expect all of you to be gone from here by tomorrow.'

The Koch *thakuria* took in the situation, and he knew that he had no choice. His side was heavily outnumbered, and they were also cut off from their reinforcements, which were on the other side of the Brahmaputra River. It would therefore be suicide to resist the Ahoms. The Koch soldiers left Sola Fort and crossed over the river in a boat to the north bank of the Brahmaputra River.

It was around this time that three brothers of Nar Narayan were on a pilgrimage to a large and deep river pool near Tezu in the east; this pool was identified by the Hindus with Brahmakunda. The three Koch royals Dip Singha, Hemadhar, and Ram Chandra were each accompanied by a thousand Koch *paiks*. A *hazarika* commanded a force of 1,000 *paiks*, and the three princes together were accompanied by a considerable force of 3,000 *paiks*. As they reached the north bank of the river Brahmaputra opposite to Sola Fort, they were met by the pathetic *thakuria* and his *paiks*, who had just vacated the Sola Fort for the Ahoms. The *thakuria* narrated the incident of confrontation with Bar Sandikai, and on hearing this, the brothers of Nar Narayan became incensed and sought to take revenge. The three Koch princes, who were in a haughty mood, ordered the Koch *hazarikas* to recover the Sola fort from the Ahoms.

The *hazarikas* proceeded across the Brahmaputra River, and initially they captured the boat belonging to the Ahom Bar Sandikai, then they proceeded further and drove out the Ahoms from Sola Fort. The Ahoms were humiliated and they had to retreat. The three triumphant Koch princes thereafter proceeded on their pilgrimage to Brahmakunda near Tezu.

The Ahoms, who had retreated temporarily from Sola Fort, were not going to take things lying down, and they prepared to ambush the three Koch princes when they returned from Brahmakunda. Sometime later, a large force of Ahoms, intent on extracting vengeance for the humiliation inflicted on them earlier, waylaid and ambushed the three Koch princes, who were on their way back from Brahmakunda. The forces accompanying the Koch princes were defeated in the battles that followed, and the three princes were also killed in the conflict.

The news about these events came as a shocking blow to Nar Narayan at Kochbehar. The grieving Nar Narayan gathered troops immediately and proceeded towards Narayanpur in the east on hearing the sad news about the loss of three of his brothers in the battle with the Ahoms.

Nar Narayan found that the movement of his army was very slow because of the difficult terrain, rivers, swamps, and jungles.

The group of advance Koch troops who were scouting the position in front came back to the main force and reported to Nar Narayan that they would have to make a detour slightly towards the foothills of the Himalayas to avoid a very large swamp which lay in front of them. This was only one of the many instances when they had to make changes in the direction of movement due to various natural obstacles on their way as they progressed further, and Nar Narayan found the progress extremely difficult and frustrating. He spoke out his thoughts to his brother Kamal Narayan, who was accompanying him, stating that if their progress was impeded in this manner time and again, they would never be able to move their men and provisions fast enough in this region. They would have to think of a solution to overcome this situation.

Kamal Narayan, who was also known as Gohain Kamal, was an enterprising man, so he thought about the challenge that faced them and later came up with the proposal of constructing a raised highway by engaging a large number of workers and sufficient resources to undertake the project. When Nar Narayan was informed about the proposal, he was enthusiastic about it and promised to support Kamal Narayan's project with the men and material that were required to complete it. He instructed Kamal Narayan to start work on the project without delay, and he further told him to construct the highway from Kochbehar in the west up to Narayanpur in the east.

This momentous decision to build an embanked road from Kochbehar in the west to Narayanpur Fort in the east would prove to be one of the most important decisions taken by the Koch king Nar Narayan and which indirectly enabled him to increase the power and prosperity of the Koch kingdom. Kamal Narayan engaged a number of supervisors and thousands of workers to build the embanked road. The work started from near Kochbehar with a small ceremony to bless the project. The workers were given sufficient incentives and extra provisions, and the supervisors made them work hard for long hours to speed up the construction of the road. The alignment of the road was deliberately kept along the submontane region adjacent to the foothills of the Himalayas. This alignment had two advantages: one was that they could avoid the low-lying swamp areas which required a lot of earth filling, and the other was that this important project could be implemented without attracting the attention of the Ahoms, whose spies were active in the Brahmaputra Valley. The Ahoms, however, came to know about the project and were quite concerned about it.

Soon hundreds of able-bodied men and women were engaged in the construction of the embanked road. Soil was dug and raised, then compacted to give stability, and drains were dug to drain out excess water during monsoon rains. Then the road was lined and paved with bricks. The 350-mile-long embanked road from Kochbehar to Narayanpur was completed by Kamal Narayan in the year 1547. There was great rejoicing, and the Koch built a fort at Narayanpur. The Koch king Nar Narayan congratulated his brother for completing the long road in record time and named the road Gohain Kamal Ali in honour of his brother Kamal Narayan's great achievement. It was quite a marvel of engineering for those days, extending around 350 miles, and this road became very useful for quick movement of troops and provisions for the Koch army and for efficient communication with different parts of the region, which later came under the control of the Koch kingdom.

The Ahoms were alarmed at this development, and the Ahom king Suklenmung decided to do something to negate this progress made by Nar Narayan. So while the Koches were rejoicing and congratulating themselves at Narayanpur on their great achievement of successfully completing the Gohain Kamal Ali Highway from Kochbehar to Narayanpur, the Ahom king surreptitiously moved a strong Ahom force to Pichala, which lay between Narayanpur and Kochbehar, and effectively blocked the communication between the Koch forces stationed at Narayanpur and their reinforcements and provisions from Kochbehar. It was a good position from which a strong and disciplined force could easily withstand enemy forces as well as inflict damaging attacks on them. The Koch king Nar Narayan sent his *hazarikas* to attack Suklenmung, who was encamped at Pichala, and the Koch *hazarikas* marched with their *paiks* towards Pichala to take on the Ahom forces led by Suklenmung. For the Koch *paiks* who went to confront the Ahoms at Pichala, the experience that followed was like walking into the mouth of a tiger. The waiting Ahoms slaughtered the Koch *paiks* as they reached the fort of Pichala. More of them were picked off by arrows from Ahom bows as they tried to escape from the terrible slaughter, and hundreds more drowned in the river. The victorious Ahoms marked their victory in a brutal manner by beheading the corpses of the slain Koch *paiks*; these were carried as trophies to a place near Sibsagar and made into one large gruesome heap at a site which thereafter came to be known as Mathadang.

CHAPTER 7

WAR DRUMS OF THE EAGLE KING

A number of years passed after the battle at Pichala, in which the Ahoms had given a licking to the Koch forces, and during these years Nar Narayan had gradually built up the strength and capability of the Koch kingdom, and his brother Sukladhvaj had also gained experience in battle as commander-in-chief of the Koch forces. With more experience, Sukladhvaj became very professional, strong, and swift in his military operations. The hallmark of his strategy in battle was that of attacking his enemies with great speed and cunning, thereby catching his opponents quite unprepared, and this tactic of his was compared to the swiftness of an eagle attacking its prey. This unique fighting style earned him the famous name of Chilarai, or the Eagle King.

There were changes taking place on the south bank of the Brahmaputra River, and this had been brought about by the Koches, who had over the years slowly but surely spread their influence and power eastwards along the valley of the river Brahmaputra. They met the first challenge to the spread of their influence from the Kacharis, who were extremely hostile to the Koch troops who suddenly started encroaching into traditional Kachari-inhabited areas. The Kacharis at this time were allied to the Ahoms, and they defied the Koches and even challenged them. The Koch *paiks* then decided to teach a lesson to the Kacharis, and they attacked and devastated a number of Kachari villages, killing and injuring several people, plundering and burning down many houses. This act of the Koches led to fresh hostilities between the Koches and the Ahoms in 1562.

The Koches had by this time also made a strategic alliance with the Bhutanese and the Nyishis who inhabited the mountainous region to the north and east of the Koch kingdom, and the Bhutanese and Nyishis had a mutually beneficial arrangement with the Koches. This relationship had grown out of the necessity of trade and commerce. In those times, there existed a very important trading route between Tibet in the north and Bengal in the south through Bhutan and the Koch kingdom. The goods that came down from the mountains included musk, Tibetan horses, and wool, and the goods that went up from the lowlands included cotton cloth, broad cloth, tools, salt, spices, and tobacco. Nar Narayan took advantage of the existence of these age-old economic ties, knowing fully well that the smooth functioning of this commercial activity depended on the goodwill of those who used this route regularly and the inhabitants of the places through which the trading route passed. They needed to cooperate with each other for their own well-being and continued prosperity. Nar Narayan now asked for the cooperation of the Bhutanese in his operations against the Ahoms, and he promised that in return the trading route through Kochbehar would not be disturbed.

The Bhutanese were Buddhists and revered the Buddha and tantric guru Padmasambhava, also known as Guru Rinpoche. The code of *driglam namzha* governed their disciplined behaviour and mode of dressing in public, in pursuance of which their men wore a heavy knee-length robe known as the *gho*. The Bhutanese soldier wore the *gho* and carried a sword and bow and arrows, and some of them carried muskets obtained through barter from the Tibetans and from the Chinese. It was usually not in the nature of the Bhutanese to interfere in other people's affairs, so initially when they received the proposal from Nar Narayan, they were reluctant to offer assistance or get involved. However, the Koch king was insistent, and he sent Chilarai to discuss and negotiate with the Bhutanese. Finally, however, the Bhutanese gave in to the arm-twisting tactics of the Koch and agreed to support Nar Narayan in his campaigns and gave a pledge to send whenever required several thousands of warriors with provisions to join his forces and to fight under the command of Chilarai.

Nar Narayan also entered into a similar arrangement with the Nyishis, who occupied territories adjacent to and east of Bhutan. The Nyishis were a slightly more wild and vigorous community. They were animists by faith and revered Abo-Tani, the primal ancestor of animist tribes. The Nyishi warriors were attired and armed quite differently from the Bhutanese. The Nyishi warrior's hair was kept long, usually plaited, and over this plaited hair he wore a cane helmet surmounted by the beak of the great Indian hornbill, and this outfit gave him a unique appearance and presence in the field. The Nyishi warrior also wore cane rings on his arms, legs, and around the waist. His chest and back were covered by buffalo hide, over which he wore a black cloak made from some sort of indigenous fibre. The Nyishi warrior's armaments consisted of a spear with an iron head, a large dao in a bamboo sheath, and a bow with arrows whose sharp tips had been dipped in *umiyu*, a kind of poison made from wild herbs.

With the joining of the Bhutanese and Nyishi troops, the composition of the Koch forces attained a kind of variety and flexibility and thereby also increased the size and striking capabilities of Chilarai's armies. This formidable combined force advanced to engage with the Ahoms, and they proceeded along the newly constructed Gohain Kamal Ali, towards Narayanpur in the east.

Chilarai had made a study of the tactics used by the Ahoms, and he was not going to take any chances this time. He organized a fleet of large boats and loaded these boats with fighting men. These boats then quickly moved upriver on the Brahmaputra River. On the banks of the Brahmaputra and parallel to the movement of the boats, a huge army comprising of Koch, Nyishi, and Bhutanese troops moved on land.

At the sight of the huge horde of ferocious troops approaching his township, the *gomatha* of Narayanpur trembled with fear, and on being challenged by the Koch warriors, he capitulated, immediately making his peace with Chilarai, and became an ally of the Koch king Nar Narayan.

Chaopha Sukhampha, the wily king of the Ahoms, was kept informed about the progress of Chilarai's huge force by Ru Rim, the top commander of the Ahom army. Ru Rim sent his spies and scouts to watch the movement of the Koch horde and inform about their activity. These Ahom scouts kept up with the movement of the Koch troops but were careful to be discreet and to keep out of sight as far as was possible, and they sent reports to their chief Ru Rim from time to time. After hearing about the strength and preparedness of the Koch forces, Sukhampha thought that it would not be wise to meet the enemy head on. He discussed strategy with his top commander.

'Nar Narayan has a combined army of Koch, Nyishi, and Bhutanese troops, but the Koches comprise the largest and dominant component of the army. Find out their habits and traditions so that we can find a weak point in their armed forces. The Koches are mostly Hindus who have great reverence for Brahmins, who have taught them about religion, and the Brahmans revere cows. We must make use of their traditions and belief in our strategy to manoeuvre and take them on,' advised Sukhampha. Sukhampha then decided to use a grand deception as his strategy to fight Nar Narayan.

The Ahoms were well aware that the Koch royal families were orthodox Hindus and had great veneration for Brahmans and cows. The Ahoms therefore dressed up a large number of their soldiers in the traditional garb of Brahmans and mischievously pulled up the sacred Brahman thread up to their ears for visibility, and these fake Brahmans were sent riding on many cows towards the approaching combined force of the Koch king. The advancing Koch scouts came in contact with these Brahmans riding on cows, and they were quite surprised and amused at this ridiculous sight. Their numbers were so large that the movement of Nar Narayan's army was impeded. On enquiry, the fake Brahmans mounted on cows informed that they were on a pilgrimage to Kashi. The scouts reported this development back to the Koch *hazarikas*, who withdrew their forces immediately and consulted the Koch king. The Koch king was confused by the situation and called his court astrologers, who were mystified but unanimously opined that the signs were not in favour of proceeding with the invasion. Reluctantly the expedition of the combined force was called off. It was only later that the Koches realized that the Ahoms had played a trick on them, for which they had fallen. The fuming Koch leaders felt foolish and itched to get their revenge on the Ahoms, but they had to wait for another year before they could regroup their troops to move against the Ahoms.

In 1563 Chilarai was assigned with the task of leading the Koches and their allies against the wily Ahoms. The first thing that Chilarai did was to summon all the commanders and troops to a great gathering, which was held in a vast open plain which could accommodate the large number of troops gathered on the occasion. The war drums of the Koch started rolling out an ominous beat, summoning the troops and their commanders, and they came from every village, township, and locality to gather in the plain. The information about the congregation was also heard by the Bhutanese and the Nyishis who were allied to the Koch, and the Bhutanese and Nyishi warriors arrived soon after with their provisions and weapons. A great feast was held for the gathered host, and on the third day of the assembly they were addressed by the Koch king Nar Narayan and his commander-in-chief, Chilarai. The address to the gathered host of troops and their commanders was not long, and the message was simple and clear: it was a call for setting out boldly on a new adventure in the shape of a campaign against the Ahoms. Immediately after the address, Chilarai separately called all the commanders for a meeting, where a detailed action plan was prepared and the *hazarikas* and *saikias* were given specific tasks. In the next few weeks after the gathering of the great numbers of men, the troops were trained for their operations. Chilarai had planned his move carefully, and he obtained complete cooperation from the Bhutanese and the Nyishis. A large number of big boats were constructed; these were not only made for carrying groups of *paiks* with weapons and provisions but were also fashioned for fast movement and easy manoeuvres in the river. These boats were meant for carrying armed troops specially trained for naval warfare. Months later the preparations were completed, and the commanders and their troops were impatient to move east for their mission. Chilarai felt comfortable with the level of preparedness of the troops; he felt that they were now ready to take on the formidable Ahoms. However, before moving off on the campaign against the Ahoms, Chilarai retired to a secluded place for his customary practice of meditation, the transcendental meditation which was said to take him on a flight of imagination. He was known to sometimes resort to this very special form of meditation before embarking on some journey or some task which he considered to be very important. Even on that day, in the very quiet and private place that he had chosen where no one was allowed to disturb him, Chilarai squatted comfortably on a small thick mat and began his meditation. He closed his eyes, relaxed the tense muscles from the top of his head to the tips of his toes, and after quite some time his mind became still, and it was lifted to the zone of transcendental meditation. At this level of meditation Chilarai transformed into an eagle in his mind once again, and this time, he was soaring through the air high above the valley of the Brahmaputra River, and as the eagle flew towards the direction of the rising sun, its sharp scrutiny was cast over the valleys, rivers, and hills of the region. The high mountains of the the Himalayas were to its left, extending in a long chain of dark ridges and shiny snow-covered peaks, and to its right the vast plains of Gauda extended to the horizon. The eagle flew on eastwards, and it reached the great bend of the river Brahmaputra, where the river took a sharp turn to the south, forming a right angle, with the direction of its flow from the east to west up to this point of the river, and then from this site, the flow of the river took a north-to-south direction. As the eagle crossed over the great bend, its sharp eyes spotted the confluence of the Jinjiram River with the Brahmahputra, and near the confluence it could make out the ruins of the City of Eastern Light, the ancient capital of Kamarupa, where once upon a time, Bhaskara, one of the greatest Varman rulers of Kamarupa, had reigned for forty-five years. Now it lay in ruins, covered with a jungle. The eagle continued to fly east, and a little later it flew over the rugged range of hills with huge rocks, known to the locals as the Staircase to the Moon. It was in the small village which could be seen faintly at the foot of this hill that Bhaskara, his brother, and his father had taken shelter as fugitives from the pursuing troops of the Gupta emperor Mahasenagupta. Continuing its flight, the eagle soon reached the Nilachal Hill; at the top of the hill could be seen the red flag at the tip of the spire of the temple of the goddess of desire, Kamakhya, which was situated atop Nilachal Hill. The eagle flew on along the course of the mighty river, and hours later it reached the site where the Subansiri River merged with the Brahmaputra. The eagle could see with its sharp eyesight that something was going on in the region, and it flew down closer to the trees and forests to get a clearer view of the activity that had caught its attention and interest. The eagle circled over the area for a while and finally flew off. Some hours later, Chilarai emerged from the place of meditation, looking relaxed and confident. Then when all things were in place for movement of the forces, Chilarai signalled to the buglers, who lifted buffalo horn bugles to their lips and sounded the launch of the campaign. With minimum fanfare the expedition set off; the main body of the troops moved east towards Narayanpur along the newly built Kamal Gohain Ali Highway, which was well made and still new. They could travel quickly and without obstructions on this new highway to the east. The fleet of boats with troops on board also sailed to the east up the river, moving more or less parallel to the army in the same direction up the Brahmaputra River. In this way, after journeying for several days, the army moving on the Gohain Kamal Ali reached the confluence of the Subansiri River with the mighty Brahmaputra River. Then the army moving on the Gohain Kamal Ali along the north bank of the river took a turn to the south and converged with the fleet of boats, which had docked on the riverbank. With the help of the boats, a major part of the forces crossed over to the south bank of the river Brahmaputra and rapidly proceeded towards Majuli and the Ahom-controlled territories. After the crossing over of Chilarai's army, the large number of boats in the river split into two fleets. One fleet of boats sailed up the Subansiri River and docked safely at a discreet and convenient location, where a camp was set up. The boats were docked on the riverside, and the troops rested and waited patiently for further events to unfold. The Subansiri was a beautiful river and was one of the largest tributaries of the Brahmaputra. It had its origins in the Tibet region, from where it followed a circuitous route flowing south-east through the Himalayas and finally turning south to flow into the lower hills, and it ultimately merged with the Brahmaputra near Majuli. The Subansiri was also famous for the gold dust that was found intermingled in the sands carried by the river. The gold miners sieved and separated this gold dust from the river sand and smelted it into gold bars which were in high demand, and it provided a steady income for these miners. Many rulers were attracted by the wealth that was generated by this process of gold mining.

The second Koch fleet, which had many more boats, plied upriver on the Brahmaputra towards the position of the Ahoms. As the second fleet of Koch boats approached Ahom territory, some patrolling boats of the Ahoms with armed men came across the approaching Koch boats and immediately gave an alarm about the presence of invaders in the river. A battle ensued in the river, and the Ahom vessels suffered heavy losses and had to turn back, as they were heavily outnumbered. The Koch forces then moved towards the Ahom positions so swiftly that the Ahoms were surprised by the speed and coordination of their deployment. The main body of Ahom troops waited cautiously on land for the Koch forces to reach the site which the Ahoms had selected for battle. The boats reached the riverbank without further incident, and the Koch troops then proceeded on land up along the slopes of the riverbank. The Ahoms silently waited to ambush them as they drew closer to their position. Chilarai studied the position of the Ahoms and decided to adopt a move close to what the Ahoms were probably expecting them to take. He sent a large force under *hazarikas* to proceed along the path that led to the site of the ambush that the Ahoms had laid for them. As they proceeded, the Ahom scouts who were keeping a watch on their movements reported back to Ru Rim that events were unfolding as per their plan. Unknown to the Ahoms, however, Chilarai secretly took a select contingent of Koch soldiers and swiftly moved south in the direction of the hills inhabited by the Naga tribes. Then on reaching near the foothills, this group of troops led by Chilarai changed direction again, and taking a sharp turn, they proceeded under the cover of forests and thick jungle towards Garhgaon, the Ahom capital, approaching it from a difficult and unexpected direction. In the meantime, the Koch forces under the *hazarikas* who had been proceeding towards the Ahom ambush site came under heavy attack. They faced small cannon fire; swarms of arrows rained down on them, and as they tried to take shelter from the heavy fire, the Ahom cavalry charged towards them. The Ahom commanders concentrated their full attention on the battle at hand, and they found that though they had the advantage and choice for the site of the battle, even then the Koch forces, who were at the receiving end, had responded immediately. The Koch army would not be defeated so easily. The Koch commanders and their troops gave a good account of themselves; they defended themselves from the swarm of arrows by lifting together their strong, rounded rhino-hide-covered shields, forming an impenetrable wall, while the Koch archers retaliated, sending swarms of arrows towards Ahom positions. Other troops quickly made barricades and dug shallow trenches for temporary shelter and defence. They withstood the most ferocious attacks of the Ahoms in a disciplined manner though they suffered losses, and whenever they were able to retaliate, they gave as good as they got. Their retaliatory attacks were sometimes successful in stinging and cutting the Ahom forces deeply. The fighting continued to rage on for hours and several days, with losses on both sides. At the close of every day, the Ahom commanders gave their report to Ru Rim, and the commander-in-chief in turn gave a briefing to Chaopha Sukham, the Ahom king, and his council of ministers. Chaopha Sukham was quite confident about the capabilities of the Ahom armed forces, and he was quite keen to know about the progress of the battle, and this he sought from the *ru rim* of the Ahom forces. The commander-in-chief of the Ahom army was not all that sure or confident, and he responded in a guarded manner to the query of the *chaopha*.

'Chaopha! Chilarai's *paiks* appear to be well trained and equipped, and they are very persevering. We have been able to stop their progress towards Garhgaon for now, but it may require a few more days of determined fighting to drive them back to Kochbehar.' Ru Rim was not one to underestimate the strength of his enemy. In fact, he wished that his own troops were as disciplined as the Koch *paiks*, who had shown great courage and resilience in spite of the fact that they were outnumbered and put at a disadvantage by the Ahom ambush. Ru Rim felt that his own Ahom soldiers had become soft and less disciplined in the fertile valley of the Brahmaputra, where they had become used to an easy life.

On hearing the report from Ru Rim, Chaopha Sukham and his council of elders were satisfied that for now at least the Koch invaders had been stopped from making further progress. On reflecting about their current situation, Chaopha Sukham felt that it was very fortunate that his predecessor, Chaopha Suklenmung, had founded and built up Garhgaon as a strong headquarter from which the Ahom dynasty could function and operate effectively. Suklenmung, predecessor of Sukhampha, had established Garhgaon as the chief town of the Ahom kingdom; he had built it up as a fort city, and the structures in the fort city were mostly made up of wood, bamboo, and stone. It was strongly built, and the Kareng Ghar, or the royal palace, was one of the main attractions of the city. In the days of Chaopha Sukham, the city of Garhgaon looked like a large circular aggregation of villages, and it did not have a wall surrounding it. Instead of a wall, the city was surrounded by a close and extensive growth of strong bamboo forest which grew in a continuous stretch around the city. The Kareng Ghar, the king's palace, was located more or less in the centre of the city. On the outskirts of Garhgaon there were four gates corresponding to the north, south, east, and west directions, and each of these gates was made with stone and set in clay. From each of these gates there was a broad raised embankment which led in a straight path up to the Kareng Ghar. The Kareng Ghar was protected by a sloping embankment on which bamboo clumps had been planted close together, forming an almost impregnable wall. The whole structure was not unlike a cosy nest made by some creature of the forest. Surrounding the embankment around the Kareng Ghar was a moat filled with water. Surrounding the raja's palace and beyond the spacious garden of the Kareng Ghar were the mansions of Ahom nobles and high officials. These houses were built on raised wooden platforms which rested on pillars of strong seasoned wood which kept the buildings above the damp ground. The houses had thatch roofs and beautiful decorative wood carvings on pillars. In the raja's palace there was a large audience hall known as the *solang ghar*.

In the *solang ghar* of the royal house, Chaopha Sukham and a large number of Ahom nobles had gathered, and they were discussing the developments following the Koch attack, and they took stock of the situation, made plans for defence and battle. This went on for some time, after which they dispersed from the *solang ghar*. They were all quite oblivious to the fact that Chilarai, with his special contingent of Koch troops, had by now reached a location quite close to Garhgaon from an unexpected route, and they were unnoticed in a hidden location, silently waiting to launch the attack on Garhgaon. Even as the inhabitants of Garhgaon prepared to retire for the night, the Koch warriors gazed at the lights of Garhgaon quietly from a hidden spot at some distance from the town. Their movements had been very cautious, and so far no one was aware about their presence at the doorstep of the Ahom capital. Chilarai examined the defences of Garhgaon carefully from the cover of trees and bamboo on an overlooking hillock; he could make out the four gates to the city, the wall-like bamboo plantation, and the moat filled with water. He called his commanders and discussed with them the strategy for attacking the fortified city. Four groups were formed; each group would attack the city through one of the four gates. It would be a four-pronged attack. One group comprised the wild Nyishi tribesmen from the eastern mountains; they were given the eastern gate. The second group comprised the Bhutia soldiers sent by the ruler of Bhutan; they were placed at the western gate. The two other groups comprised Koch *paiks* led by fierce and experienced commanders, and these would move into Garhgaon from the north and the south gates. Each of the groups had its task cut out, and the secret codes and signals for the entire operation had been intimated to the commanders of the groups. At a very late hour on that night, when almost all the lamps and torches in Garhgaon had been put out and the sounds of activity made by people in their homes became quiet, the Koches moved in closer and took positions. Still they waited patiently for the signal to launch the attack. They were like hawks that hovered in the sky, looking for an opportune moment to swoop down on unsuspecting prey, and they waited till the first crow of a rooster was heard from Garhgaon. It was still dark and only a hint of the pale light of dawn was evident on the horizon when Chilarai gave the signal for the troops to move to the gates. There was a quiet rustling sound, like the whispering of breeze through leaves, as each of the four groups of warriors immediately rushed from cover towards the assigned gate in a silent crouching jog. Every one of the gates to the approach roads was guarded by a team of Ahom soldiers, who at this hour were either asleep or at the lowest ebb of wakefulness and alertness of mind. The attackers pounced on the Ahom guards swiftly and overpowered them. However, some of the guards were able to raise an alarm and put up a stiff resistance before they were overcome. The commotion at the gates alerted the guards in the Kareng Ghar, and they immediately rushed to warn Chaopha Sukham and others. Fortunately for Chaopha Sukham and his nobles, the alert Ahom soldiers in the Kareng Ghar had reacted quickly when the alarm had been raised at the approach gates of Garhgaon, and now they activated the emergency plan which had been put in place for just such a situation.

The Ahoms had prepared a secret underground passage that connected the Kareng Ghar in the middle of Garhgaon with an isolated hidden spot in the countryside on the outskirts of the township, which was the route for escape when all hope was lost. Now Chaopha Sukham, his family members, and many important Ahom nobles and their family members hurried through this underground passage even as the Koch, Bhutia, and Nyishi warriors moved into Garhgaon along the raised embankment, proceeding towards the Kareng Ghar. As they progressed forward, the Koch unleashed fire, arrows, and missiles on the Ahom soldiers, who rallied to organize a defence of the Kareng Ghar.

Even as the Ahom soldiers shouted out the alarm again and again, Chilarai gave the prearranged signal for the first wave of attack. The high-pitched scream of the black eagle rang out through the dark night, and the Koch archers took up their bows and launched a shower of flaming arrows towards the Ahom settlements. The flaming arrows arched through the air in unison and lit up the night sky. As the flaming arrows arched downwards to the ground, some of them landed on thatch roofs, which started burning, and sometime later the sleepy occupants of the burning houses tumbled out, screaming wildly. The flaming arrows continued to rain down on the houses in Garhgaon till almost half the city was in flames.

Then once again Chilarai gave a second signal, which unleashed the second line of attack. The high-pitched cry of the black eagle rang out once again, and the Koch archers raised their bows and launched a shower of screaming arrows. These were specially made arrows with a small hollow in the arrowhead which produced a shrieking sound when air was forced through the hollow as the arrows flew through the air. As these special arrows arched through the night sky, they raised a collective shrieking howl, and this sent a chill through the hearts of the defenders and inhabitants of Garhgaon, many of whom were killed or injured by the arrows which rained down on them. This was immediately followed by the third wave of attack in which the Koch *paiks*, Nyishi warriors, and Bhutia soldiers went charging in on horses and on foot with their muskets, spears, swords, and axes, raising blood-curdling war cries and at the same time shooting with muskets and releasing more arrows to cut down the defenders. After the initial fight, which lasted for some hours, there was very little resistance, and Chilarai's soldiers stormed the Kareng Ghar, only to find to their bitter disappointment that the birds they were after had flown to safety.

This had taken place some hours earlier, even as the Koch warriors were proceeding from the gates on the outskirts of Garhgaon towards Kareng Ghar, unleashing wave after wave of fire and fury on the

Ahoms. The alerted Sukhampha, his nobles, and his followers had hurriedly rushed out of the city through the underground passage that connected Kareng Ghar to the outskirts of Garhgaon.

The escaping Ahoms, led by Sukhampha, came out at the other end of the underground passage like rats escaping from flooded tunnels, and having escaped from capture and annihilation at the hands of the Koch troops, they immediately proceeded in the direction of the Naga Hills, which was not too far off.

Even as Sukhampha was escaping with his supporters towards the Naga Hills, the Koches occupied Garhgaon, and the Ahom nobles and soldiers who had stayed back to fight on now fled towards the mouth of the Dikhow River and boarded whatever boats available in an attempt to escape. However, as the fleet of Ahom boats left the banks of the river and set out, they came under attack from a fleet of Koch boats which suddenly appeared from an unexpected direction, and a fierce naval battle took place in the river. The Koches increased pressure on the demoralized Ahom troops, who were now left without leaders who could rally and mobilize them to effective resistance. The Koch boats that had intercepted the escaping Ahoms were a part of the fleet which had been secretly docked and waiting on the banks of the Subansiri River near Majuli. The Koches had waited till the Ahom boats were well into the Brahmaputra and had reached a point where it would not be possible for them to flee back to the riverbank easily from the pursuing Koch barges. The

Koch *hazarika* in charge of the fleet had watched as the Ahom boats pushed out into the river, and he waited till they had reached far enough out on the river according to his estimation, then he asked one *paik* to wave the red flag, which was the signal for the attack. With a great roar that emerged from the throats of a thousand Koch *paiks* who were on the waiting boats, the fleet of boats which had stayed undercover so far now moved out into the river in unison to engage the Ahoms.

The shocked Ahoms realized that their progress was blocked and immediately ordered the boatmen to change direction and ply downriver and row hard with the flow of the river. As they desperately manoeuvred to turn around and change direction, the Koch *paiks* in the rapidly approaching boats fired muskets and sent showers of arrows towards the Ahom boats. Some of the arrows and cannon balls found their targets and struck down a few of those who were on board the Ahom boats, but the Ahoms still persisted in their struggle to get out from the trap laid by Chilarai's boats. After a while it appeared that the Ahoms would be able to outdistance the pursuing Koches as they began to draw away from their pursuers rapidly.

Alas for the Ahoms, there was another fleet of Koch boats downriver on the Brahmaputra, waiting for them. The wily Chilarai had laid the trap for the escaping Ahoms. The waiting Koch boats had been placed strategically in such a way as to effectively block free movement of boats on the river. The soldiers mounted on the Koch boats now fired muskets and sent flaming arrows towards the approaching Ahom boats, and the guns and flaming arrows did tremendous damage to men and boats on the Ahom side. The Ahoms were surrounded and crushed in between the two fleets of the Koches, and some of the Ahom boats tried to wriggle out desperately and reach the banks of the river; others even tried to flee by jumping into the river and swimming away. The Koch now used their spears, along with bows and arrows, to cut down Ahom soldiers, who were completely at their mercy. There was a great slaughter both in the river and on land. In this battle, the Ahoms were completely vanquished by Chilarai's troops.

Some of the Koch commanders now remembered what had happened earlier in the battle near Pichala Fort, where the Koches had been vanquished and there had been a great slaughter of the Koch *paiks*: the Ahoms had slaughtered and beheaded the Koch *paiks* and made a gruesome heap of their heads. Now these Koch commanders instructed their troops to decapitate the heads of the fallen Ahoms and to collect the grisly trophies in one heap. Ahoms were slaughtered and beheaded, and then a horrific mound of decapitated heads was accumulated at one spot.

CHAPTER 8

WAR DRUMS CONTINUE

Victory was complete for Chilarai and the Koches. The remaining Ahom nobles in Garhgaon surrendered to Chilarai and became allies of the Koch. The *bhuyans* who were earlier under the Ahom king now switched loyalty and gave their support to Nar Narayan.

This great victory of the Koches under Chilarai and Nar Narayan over the Ahoms became known far and wide in the entire region.

Many hours after leaving the underground passage, Chaopha Sukham and his followers reached a place known as Namching. The fugitives were exhausted and hungry by the time they reached Namching late on the next day, so they were compelled to make a halt there and set up a temporary camp. The hungry fugitives ate the hastily cooked meal as if it were the most delicious meal they had ever tasted, after which they fell into the deep sleep of the exhausted. The next day, the Ahoms woke up feeling refreshed because of the temporary halt and much-needed rest and then continued their flight into the hills through winding paths and thick jungle which covered the hills inhabited by hill tribes. After a few days of journey through difficult terrain, they reached a hilly place known as Klangdoi. Here the Ahoms made a camp, which was their temporary headquarters for the next few months. It was from Klangdoi that the Ahoms negotiated with the Koch, who had made Garhgaon as a temporary camp after the departure of Chaopha Sukham.

A few months passed after the victory of Chilarai over the Ahoms, and during this time, the Koches rested and consolidated their position. The shrewd Chaopha Sukham waited for some time till he felt that it was now a suitable time for negotiations with Nar Narayan, who was still camped at Majuli. To carry out negotiations with the Koch king Nar Narayan, one important Ahom nobleman by the name of Chaophuphrang Ikhek was selected by Sukhampha and appointed as his emissary to the Koch king. On receiving this assignment from the Ahom king, Chaophuphrang proceeded to Majuli with a small escort of Ahom soldiers, bearing gifts of two gold vessels, two silver vessels, and a large silver jar for the Koch king. When the Koch guards at Majuli saw the approaching group of Ahoms led by Chaophuphrang, they immediately informed Chilarai, who instructed them to treat the Ahom leader with respect. Chaophuphrang was received graciously in the Koch camp at Majuli, and he was allowed to present himself before the Koch king Nar Narayan and his general Chilarai. The Ahom king's emissary humbly offered the gifts which had been brought and then conveyed the desire of the Ahom king for peaceful relations with the Koch king. Nar Narayan accepted the gifts and responded with his conditions; speaking directly to Chaophuphrang, he told him to convey the message to the Ahom king that if he wanted the Koches to leave Garhgaon and Ahom territories, he would have to send the sons of Chaophuphrang, Thaolungmung, Shendang, and Khamsheng, who were all important members of the Ahom royalty and elite noblemen, to stay as hostage guests in the court of the Koch king Nar Narayan. This was to ensure good behaviour and compliance of the Ahoms. Nar Narayan also gave his word that if this was done, he would leave the Ahom territories with his army. Chaophuphrang was further warned not to return to the Koch camp without the hostages.

On receiving this strong message from the Koch leader, Chaophuphrang hastily returned to Klangdoi Hill, and on reaching there, he informed Sukhampha about the conditions set by Nar Narayan for his departure from Ahom territory. Now Sukhampha was left with the hard and unpleasant task of sending the hostages to the Koch king, and this unsavoury decision was made even more difficult by the bitter opposition to these conditions, which arose from the mothers of some of the proposed hostage guests. There was some delay initially because of this; however, once the matter was resolved, Chaophuphrang was at last ready to proceed back to Nar Narayan's temporary headquarters at Majuli along with the hostages. Finally, when Sukhampha's emissary left Klangdoi Hill for Majuli along with the hostages, it was the month of Shravan, considered to be a holy month by the Hindus, and the Brahman advisors of the Koch royalty took it to be a very auspicious occasion. In addition to sending the hostages, Sukhampha also made sure that all the tributes collected by the Ahom kingdom for that year were also made over to Nar Narayan. The caravan comprising the Ahom princes riding on ponies, the royal gifts and tributes carried on bullock carts, and the unit of escorting troops led by Chaophuphrang then slowly made its way down from Klangdoi in the Naga Hills to the Brahmaputra Valley towards Majuli. The caravan, led by Sukhampha's emissary, was received by Chilarai's troops and conducted to the Koch king's camp. Shortly after the royal hostage guests were placed in Nar Narayan's custody, the Koches departed from Garhgaon and Majuli. Sukhampha then returned to his capital city, Garhgaon, after the departure of Nar Narayan and Chilarai.

Following the settlement with the Ahoms, the victorious Chilarai moved on to conquer new territories. The Koches now eyed the lands under the influence and control of the Dimasa Kachari, who were known as the children of the big river. Once upon a time the Dimasa kingdom had extended over a large region, with a prosperous capital city by the name of Dimapur, located at the foot of the Naga Hills. The river Dhansiri flowed by the side of this city, and the Dimasa, who were one of the earliest settlers in this region, considered it to be a river of gold. One of the reasons for this was that when gold miners washed and sieved the sands of this river, they obtained gold particles, which they could process and mould into gold coins and gold ingots. This river of gold originated from near the Laisang Peak in Naga Hills and meandered down from there for around 352 kilometres along a course leading south to north through a lush, green countryside rich in plants and wildlife before it flowed into the Brahmaputra River. Over a period of time, with the rise of the Ahoms, the Dimasa Kacharis had been subjugated and they had come under the influence of the Ahom kingdom, with whom good relations were maintained. So when the Koch war drums were heard approaching Dimasa land, the Dimasa king Durlabh Narayan immediately mobilized his army to resist Chilarai's troops, who were drawing nearer in a threatening manner. The Dimasa warriors put up a brave fight but were finally subdued. Durlabh Narayan surrendered and negotiated with Chilarai for a peaceful settlement. This came at a price, and Durlabh Narayan had to part with sixty elephants and pay an annual tribute of 70,000 gold mohurs as a settlement with the Koch king.

At some distance to the east of the Dimasa kingdom and across the Barak River valley was another mighty range of mountains which ran in the north-to-south direction. This was the Arakan Yoma, which touched the Himalayan range in the north then ran south for around 600 miles till it submerged in the Bay of Bengal. These mountains formed a watershed that broadly separated the Brahmaputra River basin in the Indian subcontinent from the Chindwin-Irrawaddy River basin in Myanmar. Located deep inside this mountain chain, among beautiful hills and valleys, was the small and vibrant kingdom of Kangleipak. It lay nestled in a vast valley surrounded by hills. Kangleipak was ruled by Mugyamba, a Meetei king of the ancient Ningthouja clan, which had ruled Kangleipak for many centuries. Mugyamba now heard the drum beats of the Eagle King's war drums as the Koches approached his kingdom. Mugyamba had heard about the victorious exploits of Chilarai, and he did not doubt that Kangleipak would also face the same fate as the Kacharis and Ahoms if he did not act wisely. So when the messengers of Chilarai appeared in the beautiful and fertile valley surrounded by hills, they were immediately taken to Kangla, the ancient capital of the Ningthouja kings, located on the western bank of the Imphal River, and at Kangla they were presented before Mugyamba. The messengers conveyed the message from Chilarai, and after some thought, Mugyamba accepted the proposal of peaceful relations by agreeing to pay tribute amounting to 20,000 rupees, 300 gold mohurs, and 10 elephants to the Koch king Nar Narayan. Chilarai was also glad that his troops did not have to fight on this front.

Thereafter, Chilarai's attention was drawn back west across the Barak River valley, to a high plateau that was inhabited by a people of a megalithic culture who spoke a Mon Khmer language. They were known as Syntengs or Pnars, who ruled over the picturesque

Jayantia kingdom that extended over the hills to the east of Khyriem and over a portion of the plains almost up to the Surma River to the south of the plateau. The Syntengs, who inhabited these hills, were of Mongolian origin but had been gradually influenced by the culture and religion of the people inhabiting the plains of the Sylhet region, with whom they had carried on trade for centuries. The ruling families of the Jayantia kingdom had adopted Brahmanized names and also intermarried with prominent families of the Sylhet region. In order to draw the Jayantia into the mainstream, clever Brahmans of Sylhet had invented a story that the name Jayantia originated from the shrine of the goddess Jayanteswari, an incarnation of the goddess Durga, and this tale facilitated linkages between the culture of the Jayantia with that of the inhabitants of the plains of Sylhet. The Jayantia kingdom had prospered and accumulated considerable wealth from the trading of best-quality limestone that was found in abundance in the mines located on the lower slopes of the plateau. With this prosperity the Jayantia king could procure considerable amounts of gold, with which he started striking gold coins in his name. The gold coins indicated the prosperity of the Jayantia kingdom, and this now attracted the Koches, and Chilarai sent his messengers to the Jayantia king. The Syntengs were used to the freedom that they enjoyed and the cool breeze that blew over their scenic, gentle mountains and could not imagine coming under anyone else's rule. So when Bar Gosain, the ruler of the Jayantia kingdom, heard the war drums of the Koch King approaching Jayantiapur, he became alert and anxious. When the messengers from Chilarai met Bar Gosain and conveyed to him the offer of peaceful relations on payment of annual tribute, he refused their proposal for peaceful relations on what he felt were humiliating terms. Bar Gosain's refusal was conveyed to Chilarai, and soon after that the Koch army arrived near Jayantiapur. The Jayantia army rallied to protect the kingdom from the invaders; they fought bravely, but they were thoroughly routed. Chilarai himself slew the brave Bar Gosain in the battle. After the defeat of the Jayantias, the members of the Jayantia royal family were rounded up, and Bijay Manik, the son of the vanquished Bar Gosain, was produced before Chilarai. Bijay Manik was given the choice of immediate execution or submission to the Koch king Nar Narayan by recognizing him as the sovereign ruler.

The hapless Bijay Manik agreed to recognize the Koch king as his sovereign king. Bijay Manik was then installed as the king of the Jayantia on the condition of payment of annual tribute, and he was also banned from striking coins in the name of the Jayantia king.

Miles to the south of the Surma River lay another powerful and prosperous kingdom known as Twipra. It was ruled by Ananta, a king of the Manikya dynasty, and his kingdom extended up to the shores of the Bay of Bengal. The lineage of the Manikya dynasty was an ancient one and founded initially by Ratnapha, who assumed the name Manikya. More than a hundred kings of the Manikya dynasty had ruled since then, and Ananta Manikya was the one hundred forty-fifth king of the Manikya dynasty. Twipra was no lightweight and commanded a lot of respect in the region. Chilarai now trained his guns towards Twipra, and his messengers reached the court of Ananta Manikya to offer terms for peaceful relations. The ruler of Twipra felt insulted on hearing the humiliating terms, and in anger he had the messengers driven out of his court.

As soon as Chilarai came to know about the response of Ananta Manikya and the haughty behaviour of the Twipra king, he swiftly moved into the kingdom of Twipra with his army. The Koch army invaded Twipra so swiftly that Ananta Manikya was caught unprepared, and his army was at a disadvantageous position. The Twipra soldiers were completely routed by Chilarai's troops in a fierce and bloody battle. Ananta Manikya was captured and summarily executed. Then as was their usual practice, the Koch king installed the next ruler from among the members of the Twipra royal family and imposed an annual tribute of 10,000 rupees, 100 gold mohurs, and 30 horses.

Some distance to the north of the Twipra kingdom lay the prosperous province of Sylhet, which was aligned to the sultan of Gaur, and this alliance with the powerful kingdom of Gaur gave confidence to the Patsha of Sylhet, who also maintained a strong army for the protection of his province. So when the Patsha of Sylhet heard the war drums of the Eagle King, he immediately instructed the commanders of his forces to get prepared to resist the invaders. Soon enough, Chilarai's messengers reached the patsha's palace in advance and conveyed to the patsha the terms and conditions for peaceful relations. The patsha smugly replied to them that he could not accept the terms and conditions offered by Chilarai under any circumstance. His smugness quickly turned to fear when the Eagle King's troops swiftly arrived at his doorsteps and challenged his army. The troops of Sylhet fought very hard for three days and proved to be worthy opponents of the Koch army, but the resilient Koch troops finally routed them completely; the patsha was captured and executed. The surviving family members of the patsha were rounded up and produced before Chilarai. There was information that a brother of the patsha, named Asurai, was also among the captives, so Chilarai sought him out and offered to make him the ruler of Sylhet with some conditions. Asurai humbled himself before the Koch king and was installed as the patsha of Sylhet. Asurai pledged a tribute of 100 elephants, 200 horses, rupees 3 lakhs, and 10,000 gold mohurs to the Koch king.

To the north of the Sylhet plains rose a high plateau towering over the plains. Milky-white cataracts could be seen cascading down from the hills, and blooming orchids adorned the trees on the slopes during season. These hills to the north of Sylhet and to the west of the Jayantia kingdom were known as Khyriem, inhabited by a people of the same stock as the Jayantia hills but speaking a slightly different dialect. Similar to the

Jayantia kingdom, the people of Khyriem also carried on trade with the people of the Sylhet plains and were strongly influenced by their culture and religion. The Khasi chief of Khyriem was known by the name of Viryavanta. He had heard of the fate of the surrounding rulers at the hands of Chilarai and was the least inclined to share the same fate; he therefore wisely opted for peaceful relations when Chilarai's messengers appeared before him. He pledged payment of annual tribute and became an ally of the Koch king.

Touching the northern borders of Khyriem and the Jayantia kingdom and close to the Dimasa Kachari kingdom was the small kingdom of Dimarua, which was ruled by an enterprising Garo chief by the name of Panthesvar. The small kingdom of Dimarua became somewhat significant, as it was located at the crossroads of important routes leading from the western parts of the Brahmaputra Valley to the eastern parts and also vital routes connecting the valley to the hilly tracts in the eastern corners of the region and proceeding further to the Dimasa Kachari kingdom and beyond. Travellers, traders, armies, pilgrims, and itinerants had to pass through this place. Panthesvar was clever enough to realize that his fortunes lay in functioning as a facilitator for the movement of people and goods through his tiny kingdom, and he fully engaged his time and resources in doing only this. As a result of providing much-needed services to the travellers through Dimarua, the people were involved in various activities and were therefore economically quite well off. At the time when the Dimasa Kachari kingdom was powerful, Panthesvar helped them, but when the more powerful Koch king arrived at the doorsteps of Dimarua, Panthesvar did not hesitate to immediately extend his services to the Koch king. Thus Dimarua also became an ally and a tributary of the Koch king Nar Narayan.

Within a short period of around five years, the Koch kingdom, under the brilliant leadership of Nar Narayan and the dazzling exploits of his brother Chilarai, had become a dominant power in the region.

CHAPTER 9

AURA OF THE REFORMER

It was a warm and dry day in the lean season of the year, but the spot where Chilarai sat was cool and shaded from the strong rays of the sun, and he sat there enjoying his solitude for a while. Chilarai reflected on the events of the past few months and years, which had been filled with campaigns, battles, and adventure. He had no cause to complain. His brother Malladev, now better known as Nar Narayan, the king of the Koch kingdom, had made him the commander-in-chief of his armies, and Chilarai had led the warriors of the Koch kingdom brilliantly, subduing the Ahoms and the Kacharis and obtaining the submission of the kingdoms of Kangleipak, Jayantia, Twipra, and the pasha of Sylhet, the chiefs of Khyriem and Dimarua. It was therefore no wonder that his troops and followers were on a high. Almost like a bolt of lightning, they had flashed along and across the valley of the Brahmaputra River and the surrounding regions. Now the horde of Koch troops and camp followers had set up a camp on the banks of the Brahmaputra River, and there was great rejoicing with merrymaking. A little later Chilarai left his shaded spot below the trees and joined his colleagues, *hazarikas*, *saikias*, and others and joined in their banter and fun. They sipped rice beer and chewed on all kinds of local delicacies as they exchanged jokes and good-natured teasing. Chilarai's closest friends tried to tease him, saying that in the search for fame and fortune he had led all of them on a wild goose chase across rivers, over hills and valleys, and they were all praying that he would find a suitable consort soon so that they could cease from their rambling around and settle down peacefully. The bantering continued till late at night, and finally, Chilarai, a little weary with all the activity and merrymaking, at last left the company of his friends and retired to his sleeping quarters for the night. As he drifted off to sleep in his camp bed, Chilarai had a very strange dream. In this dream he was proceeding to a wonderful new land which was rich, green, and endowed with bountiful resources. There were trees bearing golden fruits, vast fields on which crops were growing, streams of clear water flowing by, and flowers of every colour blooming in gardens and parks. As he ventured further into this wonderful land, he saw at some distance ahead of him a mysterious and beautiful woman walking in front. She suddenly stopped momentarily and looked back at him, and he looked at her as if drawn by a magnet. He saw her voluptuous body, pouting lips, and mischievous dark eyes. With a deft and subtle feminine gesture the woman brushed back from her forehead a lock of her glossy black hair and looked at him again. Her hair was long and lustrous and flowed down smoothly to her slender waist. She smiled at him coyly and nodded her head slightly, as if to beckon him over to her. Chilarai felt powerfully drawn to the strange and lovely lady in his dream, and he quickened his pace as he went forward to catch up with her. As Chilarai raced forward faster and faster to catch up with the attractive woman, she seemed to draw farther away. Soon he was panting, and sweat poured down his face as he struggled to catch up with the woman. In the midst of his efforts, Chilarai suddenly saw to his right side a huge black serpent approaching him sinuously; the monster moved amazingly fast and soon blocked his way forward. Chilarai drew his sword to strike at the serpent's head, but it quickly slid away, moving around to encircle him in its coils. The huge serpent swiftly coiled itself around his legs, thighs, and torso and began to tighten its muscles, squeezing the breath out of Chilarai. He was helpless in the grip of the dark and slithery behemoth; his grip on the sword became weakened, and the sword fell from his outstretched hand. Chilarai cried out for help, struggling to get out of the serpent's grip, but there was no one to help him, and the serpent slowly turned its head to look at its prey. It became very still as it positioned itself for the final strike and drew its neck back, the muscles of its neck and body contracting like a coiled spring. Chilarai knew that it would open its mouth wide and stretch out its fangs and strike him with lightning speed. He looked at the snake's hypnotic eyes, helplessly waiting for the end to come, when suddenly the face of the mysterious woman appeared near the serpent's head. She looked concerned and frightened; he could see fear and hurt in her eyes. The serpent hesitated and stopped, and just at that moment the mysterious woman stretched out her hand to Chilarai; their hands touched, and she gripped his hand firmly and pulled him out of the serpent's grip. Miraculously the muscular coils of the gigantic serpent loosened and released him from the suffocating grip. At this stage, Chilarai woke up from his dream with a start and gave a gasp, drenched with perspiration and breathing heavily. His chest felt as if it had been suddenly released from a vice-like grip.

The next day, Chilarai was in deep thought as he contemplated on the strange dream that had disturbed him, even though he was not a very superstitious person. Chilarai decided that he and his troops needed to take a break before embarking on new expeditions of warfare and conquest.

The leaders of the Koch horde were informed that their next destination was Kochbehar, the capital of the Koch kingdom, where they would disperse temporarily to their own homes and reunite with their families, replenishing their energy before setting out on fresh adventures. However, in view of the disturbing dream, Chilarai planned to visit the temple of the goddess of desire on Nilachal Hill on his way to Kochbehar and offer sacrifices to the tantric goddess of desire at Kamakhya Temple.

The Kamakhya Temple was known for black magic and gory animal sacrifices which sometimes included the sacrifice of human beings. In those days there was a belief in the temple of the tantric goddess that the most acceptable form of sacrifice was a man without blemish. A horrifying and closely guarded secret about the temple of the tantric goddess of desire was the existence of a class of persons known as *bhogis*, who offered themselves as voluntary victims for the sacrifice to the goddess. In view of the ultimate sacrifice which they provided, these *bhogis* were awarded with certain very special privileges of satisfying all their carnal desires during their lifetime and up to the last day of their lives, when they were to be sacrificed to the goddess. Muslim invaders had at a point in time destroyed the temple of the tantric goddess during their raid into Kamarupa. After the invaders had been repulsed, the temple was reconstructed. On the occasion of the opening of the reconstructed Kamakhya Temple, the auspicious event was celebrated by the apparently voluntary sacrifice offered by 140 *bhogis*. On that incredibly horrific occasion the 140 *bhogis*, their bodies washed and clean shaven from head to toe, their senses completely dulled with doses of cannabis mixed with a concoction of juices, had entered the sacrificial chamber one by one. In the chamber, the *bhogi* knelt down and laid his head on a large sacrificial stone. Then a lithe and strong temple priest assistant who was adept at the task of wielding the axe decapitated the head of the *bhogi*, separating the head from the rest of the body with one swift stroke of a large sharp axe. Other priests immediately placed the decapitated head on a large copper salver, while the rest of the body was removed and immolated in a huge pyre. The 140 decapitated heads on copper salvers were offered to the tantric goddess of desire, with the priests praying and chanting mantras.

As Chilarai proceeded towards Kochbehar with a plan to visit the Kamakhya Temple on the way, unknown forces worked to influence events in such a way that Chilarai was destined to meet a holy reformer who would expose him to a very different philosophy, according to which the worship of gods and goddesses was a joyful celebration of life which could be performed without the offering of animal or human sacrifices.

Thus it was that at the end of one more day of journey down the Brahmaputra Valley, the Koch horde set up a temporary camp for rest. In the quiet of the evening, as Chilarai took rest, he heard the sound of music and devotional singing emanating from a large house located near the camp. Chilarai found the music so soothing that he sent one of his men to find out who the singers were. The man came back after inquiring about the house and its occupants and informed Chilarai that Sankardev, a famed religious reformer, and his followers were camping in the house, which was actually a *sattra*, or a monastery, of Sankardev's followers. Chilarai became curious and immediately sought permission to meet the sage and to listen to his teachings. Sankardev responded by welcoming Chilarai and invited him to come over to his monastery. On receiving the invitation, the Koch general took off his warrior's dress and armour, his sword, and other weapons, and as he did this he felt as if a great burden had been removed. He washed himself then wore a clean cotton dress of the common people and walked over to the *sattra*. Chilarai was very keen to know about the philosophy and teachings of the great reformer and saint whose philosophy had touched the hearts and minds of so many people. When Chilarai arrived, Sankardev welcomed the Koch General. 'All are welcome here, Chilarai, you can take rest from your struggles. Even the eagle which has flown so high needs to take rest once in a while, do be seated, relax, and I will explain to you through my songs about the philosophy of salvation which comes through faith and prayers and not through sacrifices.'

Chilarai was made comfortable, and then Sankardev explained his philosophy about salvation through faith and prayers and not through sacrifices. Chilarai listened with rapt attention and was completely fascinated by the teachings of Sankardev. It was quite different from what he had been exposed to all his life. Since childhood, he had seen pundits performing complicated rituals and pujas with the use of fire, water, and the liberal provision of all kinds of animals, fruits, vegetables, other goods and products as sacrificial offerings to gods and goddesses. The simplicity of Sankardev's teachings touched the heart and soul of Chilarai the warrior and brought about a subtle change in his perception of life and the society in which he was living. Some deep inner chord of his soul was touched even as Chilarai listened to the teachings of Sankardev and concentrated his entire mind on the meaning of the message. The public image of the great Koch general was that of a predatory eagle, swift, cunning, and merciless in his attacks on his enemies. A predator whose movements were silent and undetected till it made its final move, which was always swift, irresistible, and almost always ended with the death of the prey. This was the image that had earned him the name Chilarai, or the Eagle King. Beneath this fearsome exterior was a simple man with a clear and uncomplicated way of life, a prince who could charm his way into the hearts of men and women with his sincerity and warmth. This softer side of Chilarai was brought to the forefront under the influence of Sankardev, the renowned reformer.

Sankardev explained the deep meanings of the devotional songs even as his disciples sang them, and the male monks performed the graceful *sattriya* dances to the accompaniment of the songs. Chilarai was now deeply moved by the teachings of Sankardev. Another unlikely development that took place in the monastery of Sankardev was made possible by the presence of one attractive woman. Chilarai met this woman and was soon captivated by her every action, devotion, and movement. This lovely woman was none other than Sankardev's own niece, Kamala.

Chilarai's temporary camp near Sankardev's *sattra* stayed in place for a longer period than usual because of Chilarai's fascination for Sankardev and his teachings and perhaps to some extent due to the chemistry between Chilarai and Kamala, which over a period of time blossomed into a passionate love affair.

CHAPTER 10

SANKARDEV

The man with the aura of a saint, who had touched the minds and hearts of many people, including Chilarai, with his philosophy, was known as Sankardev. Sankardev was born in a prominent *bhuyan* family in the village of Alipukhuri, which was located near Bordowa in the Nowgaon area. Sankardev tragically lost both his parents when he was very young, and he was therefore brought up by his grandmother Khersuti, a kindly old lady. Sankardev was a talented child, and he displayed poetic and literary abilities of a high order at a very early age, and he also loved music and musical instruments. He was also amazingly fit and healthy and sometimes performed physical feats which surprised people. As a youth, one day he swam across the river Brahmaputra with ease at the height of monsoon when the river was in spate. Sankardev also showed signs of interest in spiritual matters. On becoming a young man, he got married and started looking after the affairs of the family, including the vast family property, but unfortunately, his young wife died of some illness. Sankardev was heartbroken and dejected for some time, and then his interest in spiritual matters became heightened. He concentrated more and more on spiritual matters and started neglecting his work as a landlord and gradually shifted these responsibilities to a close relative. Then one day, along with seventeen other companions, he proceeded on a pilgrimage which lasted for twelve long years. During this pilgrimage, Sankardev and his companions visited almost all the important places in the Indian subcontinent that were associated with the veneration of Vishnu. During this long pilgrimage, Sankardev was exposed to the teachings and principles of great Hindu saints and leaders, which probably influenced the development of Sankardev's own philosophy. After twelve long years, Sankardev returned from the pilgrimage with a mission in his mind: this mission was a religious and cultural philosophy that had evolved in his mind, and this new philosophy started to grow and mature in his thoughts. Being fond of music and musical instruments, Sankardev found it very convenient and natural to use songs and music as the medium for conveying his philosophy to others. A philosophy of salvation through faith and prayers rather than ritualistic ceremonies and sacrifices was evolved, and this was quite opposite to that of ritualistic worship that was practiced by the pundits in those days. Sankardev's new religious philosophy was known as Ekasarana dharma.

Sankardev's philosophy brought him into conflict with the powerful priestly class who aided and advised kings and ruling families. In order to avoid direct confrontation, Sankardev and some of his followers who were also from the *bhuyan* community and others moved to an isolated area known as Gangmau and then later on to Dhowahat in Majuli. In Dhowahat there was a significant development in which Sankardev met Madhabdeb, who was a worshipper of the mother goddess. Sankardev and Madhadeb got into an intense debate on religious philosophy which continued for a considerable length of time, and at the end of the long debate, Madhabdeb was won over by the religious philosophy of Sankardev. From a Sakta believer he changed and became Sankardev's most faithful disciple. These events became widely discussed by people, and Sankardev's popularity increased as many people were influenced by his teachings and got initiated into Ekasarana dharma.

The priestly Brahmins known as *bamuns*, who held a powerful influence on ruling royal families during those days, felt that the Ekasarana dharma advocated by Sankardev would be a threat to their influence and power, and this made them feel insecure. The *bamuns* therefore thought of a plan to counter Sankardev's Ekasarana dharma to remove this threat to their influence and power. The Majuli area was part of the territories under the control of the Ahoms, who were led by their king, Suhungmung. The *bamuns* now complained to Suhungmung that Sankardev was advocating a philosophy that was a danger to the existing social order and that he should be stopped immediately. Suhungmung was wiser than what the *bamuns* had anticipated, and after thinking for a time on their complaint, he decided to have a debate in his court between Sankardev and the *bamuns* to settle the matter. A day was fixed for the debate to be held in Suhungmung's court, and both sides came prepared. In this debate, which took place in the Ahom king's court, Sankardev was able to successfully convince the Ahom king that his philosophy of Ekasarana dharma was not a threat to the social order. All charges against Sankardev were dropped, and he and his followers were allowed to live peacefully; however, the *bamuns*, who had lost face in the debate, became sullen and remained hostile to Sankardev.

Later on, Suhungmung expired and he was succeeded by his son Suklengmung. Once again, the *bamuns*, who had a powerful influence on the Ahom king, revived their campaign against Sankardev, and they started whispering in Suklenmung's ears against Sankardev and his Ekasarana dharma. Through their influence, the *bamuns* launched a systematic campaign of harassment against Sankardev and his followers, and they were prevented from propagating or teaching the philosophy of Ekasarana dharma. The relationship with the Ahoms deteriorated gradually till a point came when Sankardev and his followers decided to migrate to a less hostile environment away from the Ahom kingdom. They moved westwards to a place located within the

Koch kingdom, where they hoped that that they would be allowed to practise their way of worship and belief without prejudice under the broad-minded rule of Nar Narayan. They at first reached Kapalabari, but finding it to be an unhealthy swampy location, they later moved to a better site known as Sunpora. Even here, they were destined to face another challenge from their arch-rivals the *bamuns*.

The *bamuns* had always maintained a very close relationship with the Koch royals, and when they came to know about the philosophy and teachings of Sankardev, which differed from their rituals, they felt threatened. Now, a few *bamuns* fed coloured information to Nar Narayan, hoping to stop Sankardev and the spread of his philosophy. They informed Nar Narayan that Sankardev's philosophy taught hatred against the established social system and that these teachings would turn people against one another, divide and destroy the established society, and lead to anarchy in the Koch kingdom. Nar Narayan was quite concerned on hearing this disturbing piece of information and issued orders for the immediate search and arrest of Sankardev and his family members.

At this point of time, Nar Narayan was not aware about the close friendship that had developed between Sankardev and Chilarai, and fortunately for Sankardev, Chilarai came to know early that Nar Narayan had issued orders for the search and arrest of Sankardev. Knowing exactly where Sankardev was located, Chilarai immediately dispatched his men to bring Sankardev and his close followers to his own house before the men sent by Nar Narayan could find them and take them into their custody. The men sent by Chilarai rushed to the place where Sankardev had taken refuge, and they were able to take them hurriedly from there to Chilarai's house before the men sent by Nar Narayan could find them. Chilarai then informed that he had taken Sankardev and his followers into his own custody, to be produced before the Koch king. At the same time, Chilarai met his brother Nar Narayan and told him about Sankardev; he pleaded with Nar Narayan to give a hearing to Sankardev before finally deciding on what further action was to be taken against Sankardev. Nar Narayan readily agreed to this suggestion given by his brother and fixed a date for Sankardev's appearance in the court.

The day appointed for Sankardev's appearance in Nar Narayan's court arrived, and the main hall of the court was filled to capacity with curious noblemen and ladies, all agog to see the renowned Sankardev and to listen to him. The pundits were quite furious with the unprecedented popularity of Sankardev, whom they considered to be an upstart. Sankardev was well prepared for the occasion, and along with a select band of his followers, he entered the presence of the august gathering. They entered the hall, singing praises to the almighty and gently beating on dhols, with the accompaniment of timbrels and the soft ringing of small cymbals, making altogether a soothing and melodious sound. Sankardev then presented himself before Nar Narayan and made obeisance in a very humble yet captivating manner, singing a beautiful devotional song with harmonious and soothing accompaniment of instruments. After this, Sankardev introduced himself and his followers and then gave an exposition of his philosophy, Ekasarana dharma, to the accompaniment of devotional songs and dances performed by his small band of followers. The whole audience was thrilled and fell in love with the captivating performance given by Sankardev and his followers. Nar Narayan was charmed by the serene appearance and behaviour of the sage; in fact, he and a large number of his nobles were completely won over by the performance and teachings of Sankardev. Later on Nar Narayan also learnt about the love affair between his brother Sukladhvaj and Kamala, Sankardev's niece, and he obtained Sankardev's blessings to arrange the marriage between Sukladhvaj and Kamala.

Chilarai the Eagle had found his mate, and life was delightfully blissful—at least, for some time. But little did he know what fate had in store for him in the near future. Time passed and a child was born to the couple, and the days were filled with laughter and the little activities that keep new parents busy. After a length of time, Chilarai once again felt the urge to seek out new lands, and he summoned the commanders of the Koch armies. The sound of the war drums of the Eagle King was heard once again, rolling out the beats, summoning his troops to get prepared for another adventure.

CHAPTER 11

KALAPAHAR

The steady beat of the Koch war drums rolled out a message summoning the troops for duty, and this information was relayed from village to village, and the warriors arrived from the hills, valleys, and plains to gather once again in the vast plain land near Kochbehar. This time, the Koch king Nar Narayan had indicated that Chilarai should lead a campaign towards the south, into the golden land of Gaur, so called because of its prosperity and wealth.

Gaur, or Gauda, was also known as Lakhnauti, and today it is only a ruined city in the Malda district of West Bengal, close to the Indo-Bangladeshi border, but in the days of Nar Narayan and Chilarai, it was a beautiful city. This city had long ago been established by Lakshmanasena, a king of the Sena dynasty, the dynasty that had come into prominence after the decline of the Pala dynasty. Much later, Bakhtiyar Khalji, a general of Qutb-ud-din Aibak, had brought the place under Muslim rule. The Muslim sultans had retained

Gaur City as the chief seat of their power for over three centuries because of its convenient and strategic location. The city sprawled along the eastern bank of the river Ganga, stretching north to south for around seven kilometres. It was a prosperous city of more than a million citizens and was protected by ramparts which surrounded the entire city. The palace of the sultan was located in the south-west corner of the city, and it was protected by a deep moat filled with water. The city was also well known for a number of imposing structures, such as the Great Golden Mosque, with twelve doors; the Eunuch's Mosque, which had fine carvings; the Tantipur Mosque, with mouldings in brick; and the Lotan Mosque of glazed tiles.

The ruler of this prosperous city was Suleiman Khan Karrani, a sultan of Afghan origin who recognized the Mughal emperor of Delhi as his overlord. The wily Afghan sultan had heard of the exploits of Chilarai, and he had always suspected that sooner or later, the Koch would invade Gaur. So he was not surprised when his informers told him that the Koch troops were going to invade the city of Gaur. On receiving this information Suleiman told his infamous general named Kalapahar to defend Gaur from the invaders.

This man named Kalapahar had a most interesting history. He was originally Rajiv Lochan Rai, a Hindu general of the king of Odisha, Gajapati Mukundadeva. Rajiv Lochan Rai was such a capable general that he had been able to frustrate every attempt made by Sultan Suleiman to invade Odisha. It was said that one time, when Sultan Suleiman had launched a very vicious campaign against Odisha, Rajiv Lochan had led the combined forces of Mukundadeva and another king to a thumping victory over the forces of Sultan Suleiman of Gauda. Following this defeat at the hands of Rajiv Lochan, Sultan Suleiman decided to negotiate directly with him, and he sent messengers inviting Rajiv Lochan for discussions. The meeting was arranged in a grand environment where Sultan Suleiman played the role of a gracious host. Songs, dances, and cultural programmes followed the discussions and finally ended with a splendid feast. There was a lot of interaction between the hosts and their guests on this occasion, but there was one interaction which immediately caught the attention of the sharp old sultan. He observed that when his comely daughter Rukshana made an appearance in the gathering along with her friends to witness a ghazal performance, the visitors noticed her beauty immediately, and later on when Rajiv Lochan Rai and Rukshana were introduced, they seemed to take to each other at once. This chemistry between the two young people did not go unnoticed, and the wily old sultan was sure to use his imagination to make the most of it. Rukhshana's blue-green eyes, the colour of the waters of the Bay of Bengal in winter, her long dark hair, and coquettish smile completely captivated Rajiv Lochan, and he fell head over heels in love with the petite girl of Afghan lineage. Rukshana found Rajiv Lochan attractive in a virile and dashing way. The shrewd Sultan Suleiman thereafter ensured that his daughter

Rukshana was present in all subsequent negotiations with Rajiv Lochan Rai. Subsequently there were many occasions in which representatives of Mukundadeva and Sultan Suleiman met and held discussions, during which there were lengthy negotiations between the representatives, followed by breaks for food and drinks and entertainment. It was during these intercessions that more interesting interactions took place in small dispersed groups of the participants from both sides. It became quite common for Rajiv Lochan and Rukshana, the princess of Gaur, to separate themselves from the others and to continue their interaction away from prying eyes as they walked together in the pretty gardens of Gaur. They had become quite close during these interactions, and a warm and intimate relationship soon developed between the Muslim princess of Gaur and the Hindu general of Odisha. A lovely summer house made of intricately designed cane and bamboo had been constructed on the bank of a refreshing pool of water in one of the charming gardens of the city, and this site became a favourite point of rendezvous for the two lovers. Happy sounds of laughter, giggles, light talk, and other joyful noises emanated from this summer house, where further interaction and negotiations were being carried out between Rajiv Lochan and Rukshana. These developments were keenly observed by the shrewd Suleiman, who was quite satisfied with the way events were taking shape. After several days and many rounds of interaction in the summer house by the enchanting pool, it was very clear that Princess Rukshana had been charmed by the handsome Rajiv Lochan and also that she had captured the heart and soul of the Hindu general. Soon thereafter, Rajiv Lochan, completely besotted with love for Rukshana, formally called on Sultan Suleiman and asked for permission to marry the princess. Sultan Suleiman was happy with the way that things had finally turned out and agreed to the proposal of Rajiv Lochan Rai, on the condition, however, that Rukshana be converted to the religion of her husband or vice versa.

When Rajiv Lochan informed his lord and master, Mukundadeva, about his proposal to marry the princess of Gaur, the king of Odisha found it unacceptable. Mukundadeva, who had earlier ascended to the throne of Odisha through treachery and bloodshed, was also a staunch follower of Hinduism. He was not comfortable with the fact that his favourite commander, Rajiv Lochan, had fallen head over heels for a Muslim princess, and on top of that, she was the daughter of his sworn enemy. He was so much against the proposed matrimonial alliance that he got a pronouncement issued declaring that conversion to Hinduism was illegal. He further ordered that neither Rajiv nor his sons would be allowed to enter the premises of the Jagganath Temple at Puri if the marriage took place. This unexpected opposition to the marriage from Mukundadeva surprised and enraged Rajiv Lochan, who felt betrayed by his lord and master, whom he had served without any questions, faithfully for so long. Rajiv was Mukundadeva's right-hand man and commander of his armies. Obsessed and blinded by his love for Rukshana and devastated by Mukundadeva's opposition, Rajiv Lochan decided to sacrifice everything to be with his beloved, and so he defected to the camp of Sultan Suleiman along with his closest followers. The marriage ceremony of Rajiv Lochan and Rukshana took place with the blessings of Sultan Suleiman and despite strong opposition from Mukundadeva. After the marriage, Rajiv Lochan, along with Rukshana, proceeded to the holy temple at Puri to seek the blessings of Lord Jagganath, but when he arrived there, the pandas of the Puri Jagganath Temple refused them entry into the temple. When this happened, Rajiv Lochan was crestfallen and felt deeply humiliated. At this point a change took place in his mind that would send his destiny spinning in a very different direction. From that point onwards, Rajiv Lochan completely changed colour like a chameleon and became an ardent campaigner against worship of idols.

The defection of Rajiv Lochan Rai was going to be a hard blow for Mukundadeva, king of Odisha. Soon thereafter, the shrewd Sultan Suleiman felt that the time was right to once more invade Odisha. Suleiman declared that the insult to his son-in-law and his daughter could not be tolerated and that he would see that justice was done. The sultan launched another campaign against Odisha. This time, he sent an expedition headed by his son Bayazid, and the troops of Gauda were now under the command of Rajiv Lochan, who had assumed an alias. Rajiv Lochan was a powerful asset in the hands of the sultan of Gauda as he knew Odisha like the back of his hand; he knew about the strengths and weaknesses of the armies of Odisha, and he was familiar with the tactics used by them. In the battles that followed, the armies of Odisha were routed again and again, and Rajiv Lochan took his revenge on Mukundadeva and the pandas of the Jagganath temple at Puri who had humiliated him. He destroyed the idols of Balabhadra and Subhadra in the Jagganath Temple at Puri. He also ravaged the famous temples of Midnapore, the Khirachora Gopinath Temple of Balasore, the Khiching Temple of Mayurbhanj, the temples of Konark, Bhubaneswar, Jajpur, and Cuttack. Soaked in the blood and destruction of so many holy places, Rajiv Lochan Rai now emerged in a new avatar as Kalapahar, the Destroyer, the Black Mountain. He came to be known far and wide by the loathed name of Kalapahar.

CHAPTER 12

CAGED EAGLE

Thus when the war drums of the Koch were heard approaching the golden land of Gauda and Chilarai's troops appeared on the horizon, Suleiman, the sultan of Gauda, sent the infamous Kalapahar to defend the kingdom from the invaders. Kalapahar, an old hand in matters related to warfare, had kept himself informed about the events that had been taking place in the region. He knew the details of Chilarai's activities and the string of conquests made by the Koch soldiers and the tactics that were used by them. This knowledge was possible because the Kingdom of Gauda practised an ancient system of gathering information through a network of informers that comprised traders, travellers, farmers, camp followers, and harlots and even itinerant mendicants. The information gathered from these sources were used for various purposes by the rulers and other wealthy and powerful people. Suleiman and Kalapahar had all along suspected that sooner or later the Koches would attack Gauda, as they were close neighbours and there had been conflicts on earlier occasions. They were therefore prepared for an invasion from that front.

As Chilarai's *paiks* moved into Gaur, they saw before them the troops of Suleiman confronting them with a few cannons and many long spears, muskets, and bows and arrows. The forces of Gauda took the initiative in the battle by firing a few shots from small cannons at the advancing Koch troops. This did little damage to the troops but succeeded in stinging them and arousing them to rash action. As the Koches went charging in to smash the small cannons that had stung them, Chilarai and some of his commanders followed at a slower pace a little behind the charging troops. Then Kalapahar, who was intently observing the movements of the Koch invaders, sent a wing of the Gauda forces in a flanking movement. A large wing of the Gauda army, with the troops all dressed in black clothes, had been kept hidden far behind for just such a strategy, and now this flanking force of Kalapahar moved swiftly like the coils of a gigantic serpent and surrounded Chilarai and some of his commanders and *paiks* who were lagging behind. This brilliant flanking movement initiated by Kalapahar succeeded in cutting off Chilarai and his small group of men from the main body of Koch troops. Swiftly they were completely surrounded by several alternating rings of Kalapahar's infantry with long spears and trained cavalry troops on horses with swords and shields and bow and arrows. These were reinforced by the Gaur elephant cavalry. When they were completely surrounded on all sides, some of Chilarai's commanders made a valiant effort to break through the encircling rings of Kalapahar's well-trained contingent of soldiers which swelled, surged, and rotated, but these valiant men were quickly cut down. Chilarai looked left and right for an escape route but could not find one; he finally had to admit that he had been well and thoroughly outmanoeuvred, so he surrendered reluctantly to Kalapahar to avoid further bloodshed for his troops. Chilarai and a small group of his officers who had also been captured were then taken to the city of Gaur. The rest of the Koch army dispersed and returned to Kochbehar on instructions from Chilarai.

With the capture of Chilarai, the morale and fortunes of the Koch kingdom under Nar Narayan plummeted to a low level, and the war drums of the Koch kingdom ceased to sound for some time. After capturing Chilarai, Kalapahar embarked on a campaign of destruction in the Brahmahputra Valley; his army invaded Kamarupa and plundered a large number of towns and cities, causing misery for the people of Kamarupa. Even Kamakhya, the temple of the goddess of desire, was destroyed and plundered. On the way back from the campaign of devastation, Kalapahar laid siege to Kochbehar, the capital of the Koch kingdom. Nar Narayan, now at the receiving end, was hard put to defend Kochbehar from the besieging forces of Gauda, but to his good fortune some disturbing developments took place in faraway Odisha which led to the recalling of Kalapahar and his forces by Sultan Suleiman.

Kalapahar then withdrew his forces from the siege of the Koch capital and rushed back to Gauda. On return to the city of Gaur, he was sent by Sultan Suleiman on another mission to Odisha, from which he could never return.

In the meantime, Chilarai was languishing as a prisoner in the city of Gaur even though he was treated very well by his captors. In captivity, however, fate once more smiled on Chilarai. Chilarai was blessed with a charming personality, and this had not gone unnoticed by Sultan Suleiman Karrani's wife and mother, who were inexplicably intrigued by the charming Koch general who had been made famous for his exploits by his nickname of Eagle King. They secretly admired his behaviour and bearing even though he was Sultan Suleiman's prisoner in Gauda. Then one fine day, when the two begums were strolling with their friends and attendant maidens in one of the beautiful gardens of Gaur, the sultan's mother accidently stepped on a poisonous snake which lay hidden on the garden path, covered by grass and dry leaves. The startled and enraged snake bit the ankle of the unfortunate lady, who collapsed to the ground with a cry of pain and shock. Chilarai, who had been allowed to move around liberally within certain areas of Gaur, was spending some time in the splendid environment of the garden with some companions when he heard the alarm and cry raised by the maids and followers of the noble ladies, and he immediately went over to the spot to see what the commotion was all about. When he saw what had happened, Chilarai took a *gamocha* and tied it very tightly like a tourniquet around the lady's leg above the site of the snakebite to prevent the flow of poisoned blood to the heart and brain. A small cut was made on the bite wound to induce the poisoned blood to flow out, and Chilarai put his mouth to the wound, sucked out the poisoned blood, and spat it out. This was repeated several times, and it helped the sultan's mother to survive till further treatment could be given. As luck would have it, Chilarai knew of a holy man who had the skills of curing people who were bitten by snakes. This man was a learned Sufi saint who had settled in that part of Gauda, on the banks of the Ganga River. Chilarai told Suleiman about the Sufi saint, and immediately messengers were sent to summon the healer. The Sufi healer was brought by boat from his dwelling place which was located on the banks of the river Ganga. On his arrival at the sultan's palace, the Sufi healer immediately attended to the stricken lady, and he was able to treat her successfully and nurse her back to good health. This incident brought the family of Sultan Suleiman Karrani closer to Chilarai, and to his good luck, circumstances now started working in his favour. The sultan of Gauda had softened his attitude towards Chilarai much more under the influence of his wife and mother, and he even became quite friendly with him. Events were now taking another turn. 'Sukladhvaj! Your action has saved my mother from sure death, and for this I am grateful to you. You should know that we would prefer to have you as a friend rather than an enemy.'

Chilarai responded modestly, 'Sultan! I was only doing my duty as any other human being would have done, it is my privilege that I could be of some service to your noble mother.'

Under the influence of his mother, Suleiman became friendlier with Chilarai, and to bring this friendship closer, Suleiman offered the hand of one of his daughters in marriage to Chilarai, and with the marriage, the five *paraganas* of Bahirband, Bhitarband, Gayabari, Sherpur, and Dasakaunia were offered as dowry. It was a great boon for Sukladhvaj. This friendship gradually developed into trust, so much so that when Nar Narayan gathered the Koch forces and marched towards Gaur to free Chilarai from captivity, Suleiman entrusted Chilarai with the responsibility of persuading Nar Narayan to abandon the expedition.

CHAPTER 13

GAME OF DICE

The time spent by Chilarai as a captive in Gaur turned out unexpectedly to be very fruitful for him. It became an opportunity for him to learn about events that were taking place in other parts of the Indian subcontinent and how these influenced political and economic conditions in Gauda, the Koch kingdom, and the entire region. It broadened his mind and gave him a good grasp of larger regional perspective. He learnt that the sultan of Gauda owed his allegiance to the great Mughal emperor who ruled from Delhi, and Chilarai was convinced that it was in the best interest of the Koch kingdom to have strong allies in the east to consolidate its position, as there were powerful rival forces moving from the western part of the Indian subcontinent. It was therefore time for the Koch king Nar Narayan to re-examine the policy towards the Ahoms, who were at that time the strongest nation in existence, adjacent to and east of the Koch kingdom. Chilarai communicated this new line of thinking to his brother Nar Narayan confidentially, that it would be advisable in the long run to cultivate friendship with the Ahoms and strengthen ties with them.

Nar Narayan had earlier, after the significant battle in which the Ahom King had been humbled by the Koch forces, made a settlement with the Ahoms, as a result of which the Ahom king was given back his capital, Garhgaon, in return for an annual tribute and the holding of a number of family members of the Ahom king and prominent Ahom leaders as guest hostages in the court of the Koch king. These hostages were treated well by Nar Narayan, almost like family members, and quite frequently Nar Narayan played dice with Sundar Gohain, one of the hostages, who was also a prince of the Ahoms.

One day as Nar Narayan was retiring for the day, a messenger arrived from Gauda, carrying an important message from Chilarai. The message that came was regarding the need to build bridges of friendship and cooperation with his neighbours to the east, the Ahoms. Nar Narayan went through the message and immediately understood the deeper connotation of the information that had been conveyed to him by Chilarai. Nar Narayan made his own analysis of the situation and made a decision, which he put into action in the next few weeks.

Around that time, the festival of lights, Diwali, was to be celebrated, and it was a very popular festival, which was celebrated by families performing many traditional activities together in their homes. The festival also signified the victory of good over evil, and this was celebrated by the lighting of *diyas*, which are small lamps made of clay. Playing of dice and gambling during Diwali was also a common indulgence, so on that particular day, Nar Narayan cleverly arranged for a game of pachisi and invited Sundar Gohain, the Ahom prince, to play the dice game with him. It was played with one or two die, and the goal of the game was to move each of the players' pieces home to the centre space. As they started the game of dice, Nar Narayan and Sundar Gohain each selected four pieces of the same colour and placed them in their respective starting areas. The die was rolled and Nar Narayan went first. The game went on and the pieces were moved on the board. It was a festive occasion, and the game of dice was played leisurely and went along with the consuming of food and drinks as the game went on. It went on for a long time, and in the end it was Sundar Gohain who got all his four pieces home first and won the game. This was one of the few occasions when Nar Narayan lost in the game of dice, and he made a comment as the game ended.

'Sundar, you have won today on a very auspicious occasion,' Nar Narayan observed.

'I was lucky, O King, with the blessings of Goddess Lakshmi.'

'Then you must be rewarded suitably.'

Sundar Gohain smiled and agreed with Nar Narayan. He imagined that the Koch King would bestow some gift of gold or precious stones, like jade or ruby from Myanmar, as he usually did on such occasions. Nar Narayan remained silent and looked thoughtful. He did not name his reward immediately, following his normal practice. Sundar Gohain was slightly puzzled and wondered why the Koch king was hesitant in speaking out the reward this time. Finally, when Nar Narayan broke his silence and revealed what the prize would be, Sundar Gohain's face was a picture of surprise and pleasure.

'Sundar, on this special occasion, I am releasing you so that you may go back to live with your father, Chao Sukhampha, and other near and dear ones at Garhgaon. Also take with you all your followers.'

Sundar Gohain was surprised and truly overjoyed when he heard about the reward bestowed by Nar Narayan. He immediately rose up and made obeisance to Nar Narayan, putting his palms together. 'Pranam! King Nar Narayan, I will be grateful to you forever for this great kindness.'

There was great excitement when sometime later Sundar informed his friends and family members about the good news. Immediately preparations were made to leave Kochbehar for the Ahom capital. A few days later, Sundar Gohain and his followers departed from Kochbehar and set out for the Ahom king's capital at Garhgaon.

With this move Nar Narayan was able to win the friendship of the Ahom king Sukhampha, who was most grateful for the release of Sundar Gohain and his other companions from the Koch king's custody.

CHAPTER 14

THE INTRIGUE

Around the time that Sundar Gohain was released by Nar Narayan as a consequence of the game of dice, Chilarai, who was still a prisoner in the city of Gaur, had become a favourite of Sultan Suleiman so that when the Sultan's wife suggested that Chilarai be freed from captivity, the sultan responded positively. Suleiman Khan Karrani allowed Chilarai to return to Kochbehar with his blessings and urged him to persuade the Koch king Nar Narayan to maintain favourable relations with Gauda. Not only Sultan Suleiman was saddened by Chilarai's departure from Gaur. The noble begum of Suleiman, who had also developed a friendship with the brave and charming Koch warrior, felt a little melancholy when he left for Kochbehar. It was she, with her discerning sensitivity, who had known that Chilarai was feeling like a caged creature in Gaur in spite of all the kindness and honour that had been showered on him by the sultan's family. An eagle could never be happy unless it was able to soar freely in the sky above to fully appreciate its freedom.

Sultan Suleiman, who owed his allegiance to Akbar, the Mughal emperor in Delhi, had always remained loyal to his sovereign ruler. He was careful not to act in any way that would be tantamount to a rebellious act against the sovereign and which could lead to the breaking of the good relationship with the Mughals. He did not strike coins in his own name; he also honoured Akbar, the Mughal emperor, as the supreme ruler of Gauda, also known as Bengal, by ensuring that Akbar's name was read in the mosques all over Bengal during *khutbah*, the sermon at the Friday congregational prayers. This shrewd show of loyalty by Suleiman ensured that there was peace in the region between the Mughals and Bengal.

When Chilarai returned to Kochbehar on his being released from captivity by the sultan, there was great rejoicing in the Koch kingdom. The powerful Koch *karjis*, who had prospered with booty from earlier campaigns led by Chilarai, were itching for more loot and plunder, and now they tried to prevail on Chilarai to lead them once again on another campaign for more plunder and loot. At first Chilarai was reluctant and refused, but under constant pressure from some of the *karjis*, Chilarai later on relented and without much enthusiasm agreed to lead another expedition. The Koch war drums began to roll out summons to the warriors, and once again warlike preparations were started. The Koch warriors gathered to train vigorously for another campaign. After a length of time, the Eagle King moved out with a large army towards the city of Gaur, where he had earlier been held captive. Chilarai ensured that messengers were sent much in advance to Suleiman to politely ask for his submission. Suleiman, by this time, was a tired old man, and he did not wish to have fresh conflicts with the Koch; moreover his famous commander-in-chief, Kalapahar, along with many soldiers, had perished in Odisha as a result of poisoning. Sultan Suleiman, therefore, retreated with his family, friends, and important nobles and supporters to another city known as Tanda, which lay to the south of Gaur, from where he continued to rule Bengal. In the meantime, the city of Gaur was taken over by the Koch.

Not very long after the retreat to the city of Tanda, Suleiman, who was already quite old, passed away and was succeeded by his son Bayazid, who was quite a different kettle of fish from his father, Suleiman. When Bayazid Khan ascended to the throne of Bengal, a period of uncertainty and instability returned to Bengal as Bayazid immediately declared independence and broke allegiance to the Mughal emperor. Akbar, the then Mughal emperor, was busy with his campaign in Gujarat, so he decided to send his trusted officer Munim Khan, governor of Jaunpur, to stem the uprising in Bengal. Munim Khan was known to be a brilliant strategist, used to intrigues and negotiations, and in his typical style, Munim Khan initially hatched a plan to remove Bayazid from the throne of Bengal without taking to the field of battle. Munim Khan put his plan into operation by secretly sending a messenger to meet Bayazid Khan's brother-in-law, Hansu, who could be described as a worldly man without strong principles. Hansu was offered the throne of Bengal if he could take care of Bayazid, who had become a thorn in the side of the Mughals. Greed for wealth and power swayed Hansu to accept the offer, and he engaged an assassin to eliminate his brother-in-law, Bayazid. Hansu was under the illusion that with the assassination of Bayazid he could ascend to the throne of Bengal and his fortunes would be made. Unfortunately for Hansu, once the evil deed was done, he found that the nobles of Gaur would not cooperate with him. The nobles turned against Hansu for betraying Bayazid; they immediately set him aside and installed Bayazid's younger brother, Daud, on the throne of Bengal, thereby nullifying the conspiracy hatched by Munim Khan.

Daud Khan Karrani followed the example set by his brother Bayazid and declared Bengal independent from the Mughal empire. This forced Munim Khan to go to war against the obstinate Daud Khan Karrani. The governor of Jaunpur was helped in the endeavour against Daud Khan by two formidable veterans. One was Todar Mall, an able warrior who later went on to become Akbar's finance minister, and the other was Raja Man Singh, a trusted general of the Mughal emperor.

Regional alliances came into play, and the Koch king Nar Narayan entered into an understanding with the Mughals. Even as the Mughals moved against Daud from the west, Nar Narayan sent Chilarai with his troops to keep pressure on Daud Khan from the east. Chilarai, with the Koch army, harassed Daud Khan's forces from the eastern front. In the conflict between the Mughals and Daud Khan Karrani, three major battles were fought. The Battle of Patna, the Battle of Tukaroi, and finally the Battle of Rajmahal, where Daud Khan was defeated and executed.

Though Chilarai played a minor role in the subduing of Daud Khan by the Mughal forces, this did not sit well with his conscience. The fact that he had betrayed Sultan Suleiman and his gracious begum, who had treated him kindly during his captivity in Gaur, pricked his conscience, and soon after this a series of mysterious events took place which appeared to be a sign that the gods had forsaken Chilarai and withdrawn their blessings and protection from him. Chilarai now once again remembered the kindness of the noble begum of Suleiman Khan and felt just a little remorseful about the decision that had been made to turn against Gauda.

In those days, a devastating disease that caused the eruption of painful rashes on the body of those infected by it was sweeping many parts of the Gangetic plain, causing misery for thousands of people. As Chilarai and his troops moved along the banks of the Ganges River, they came across villages where people were affected by the disease, which had spread like an epidemic. The unfortunate victims of the disease were covered with rashes, dried scabs, and pustules; they had high fever and suffered terribly. Chilarai and his troops looked at them with horror and were touched by their suffering. In one particular village, Chilarai saw a little child who would be around the age of his own little son very seriously ill with the disease. The child he saw was in agony; the child's entire face, hands, feet, and body were covered with small bumps that were filled with opaque fluid, and each bump had a small depression or dimple in the centre. The profusion of small bumps that covered the eyes, lips, nose, and ears deformed the appearance of the child. The child sat alone, abandoned by loved ones who were afraid that the infection would spread to them as well. The child was in pain and cried out for water, and this pathetic sight touched the heart of the warrior who was known as the Eagle King. He got down from his horse before anyone could stop him and, pulling out a water bag, approached the sick child. His companions cried out with concern, requesting him to refrain from touching the sick child.

'Stay away from the child! The disease is very infectious.'

By this time, he had already reached the suffering child, and he knelt down by the side of the child, uncorked the water bag, and handed it to the child, who immediately grabbed it with feeble little hands and greedily drank the cool water from the water bag. Chilarai left the water bag with the little child and departed from there with his companions.

Days later, Chilarai and his troops were still on the campaign trail, keeping up pressure on the Gauda army, but it was now more or less a futile exercise, as Daud

Khan had been defeated and executed by the Mughals in the Battle of Rajmahal.

At the end of one hot and tiring day of travelling on dusty trails, Chilarai and his army halted on the banks of the river Ganga and made camp. Chilarai wiped his perspiring forehead with a light cotton *gamocha* and was surprised to feel rashes which had erupted suddenly on his skin. By evening he was slightly feverish, and he called for the *ojha*, who functioned like a camp doctor. The *ojha*, who was an experienced healer, examined Chilarai and immediately advised rest and isolation for the Eagle King. Chilarai directed his commanders to engage some troops who were skilled in wood and bamboo craft to erect a separate hut on the banks of the Ganga to accommodate him in isolation. Then he asked them to provide some food and water in the shed and asked the commanders and troops to move away to a safe distance. Brushing aside all protestations and offers of assistance, the Eagle King decided that he would fight this particular battle alone. He would either survive or succumb to the illness on the banks of the great river which he loved to watch. As he tried to make himself comfortable in the hut, he looked at the mighty Ganga River flowing by, and he remembered some of the good times he had spent along with his brother Malladev in the ashram of Guru Brahmananda in Benares. They had loved to plunge into the cool waters of the river Ganga on hot days after classes were over in the ashram. He also remembered the long leisurely walks in the evening on the sandy beaches of the mighty river.

Chilarai got up with some effort and moved to the riverside. He walked into the shallow part of the river and splashed water on himself. The water was cooling, but the rashes on his body were painful, and he felt a burning sensation. With a groan, Chilarai made his way back slowly to the hut on the banks of the river. His youthful days in Benares, which were full of fun and enjoyment, seemed to have been just a dream which he had seen so long ago.

CHAPTER 15

DANCE OF HONOUR

There was a low groan from the shed where Chilarai fought with the disease which afflicted him; it sounded painful. It was a beautifully built shed, made for shelter and comfort, and it stood on a large sandy beach on the banks of the river Ganga and looked somewhat like a summer house. Inside the shed, on a low charpoy, lay Chilarai; he was suffering miserably. The *ojha* had tried all his treatments; other herbal experts had also given him potions and mixtures of various medicinal herbs, all to no avail. Now there was no one too close to him because of the nature of his illness, and as the sickness progressed further, the fever and rashes were accompanied by pain in his muscles. Soon he had severe headache and became delirious; most of the time he was bedridden. Rashes started appearing in his mouth and on his tongue, making it an agony for him to swallow or eat anything. His back ached and he vomited frequently. His misery and pain were unending, and one could only imagine how long his body would be able to endure the suffering. In his troubled feverish sleep, Chilarai hallucinated about battles being fought by his troops, and he called out to them in a loud voice, rallying them to fight on till the enemy was vanquished or put to flight. Outside at some distance from the shed, a few soldiers stood on duty, discussing in low tones about the sick man. The most senior among the soldiers on duty was a seasoned veteran of many battles, and he was talking to the younger Koch soldiers, who listened to him with rapt attention. Most of the younger soldiers were new recruits and had not seen much real action. Many of them had joined Chilarai's army inspired by stories of adventure, action, and glory. They had been told about the legendary exploits of the man who now lay dying in the shed. It was difficult for them to imagine that the same sick and helpless person who lay writhing with pain in the hut was known as Chilarai the Eagle King, warrior and commander of the Koch hordes which had swept across the region, humbling many kings, chiefs, and armies.

The seasoned veteran narrated the story of their expedition against the Ahoms and how the Ahom soldiers, disguised as Brahmins, had pretended to be on a pilgrimage to Kashi, and this had initially deceived the Koch army, but later on the Koches had won a great victory over the Ahoms. He went on to tell them about other battles that they had fought against the Dimasa king, the king of Twipra, the raja of Jayantia, the pasha of Sylhet, and others. The Koch warrior Sukladhvaj had by then become well known by the name Chilarai, or the Eagle King, because of his incredibly swift attacks and the strategy of using surprise to unsettle the enemy and rout them in quick decisive battles. In a lower confidential tone, the veteran told the young troopers that sometimes during a battle, Chilarai would secretly turn into an eagle, and with his mystic power, the eagle guided the movements of the Koch troops in the battle, leading them to victory. Some of the other kings and chiefs, like those of Manipur, Dimarua, and Khyriem, had submitted without opposing the Koch army. The young recruits were thrilled to hear about the adventures which the older *paiks* had experienced, and they also felt that they would have followed such a leader to the ends of the world. This famous man now lay stricken with the pox, writhing with pain in a shed on the banks of the river Ganga. The soldiers became silent later on, each person immersed in his own thoughts. Each and every man was aware that if the Eagle King perished, his dreams of glory and adventure would probably come to an end.

A few days later, close friends, family members, and relatives of Sukladhvaj arrived at the site of the shed near the Ganga River, having travelled to the place all the way from Kochbehar. The information about his sudden sickness had been conveyed to them by messengers, and his near and dear ones had decided to travel immediately to the place where a rest camp had been set up for Chilarai. His beloved wife, Kamala, had also come, and she was anxious to attend to Sukladhvaj and comfort him but was restrained by others from doing so, in order to prevent infection with the same disease which had attacked her husband. Sukladhvaj and Kamala looked at each other from some distance, as if for the last time. Chilarai's face was hardly recognizable, disfigured as it was with the rashes which had erupted all over; he tried to smile at her and spoke a few words, asking her to look after herself and to take care of their son, Raghu. Kamala heard his hoarse voice as he tried to speak with much difficulty, and she wept silently as she saw him grimacing with pain, and she nodded her head slowly, acknowledging Chilarai's wishes. Kamala could not do anything more for Chilarai; she was so desperate to save him that she asked Nar Narayan to send someone to Kashi to look for a healer, and Nar Narayan had told her that he had already thought about doing just that, but he had been informed that there was no healer and no medicine for this disease, so she prayed silently for her beloved husband. She prayed that he be spared from further suffering. Chilarai also had a few words for his relatives, friends, and commanders of the Koch troops. He thanked them for being with him through every turn in his life, in the adventures and victories which they had experienced together, the joys of victories and pain of setbacks that they had experienced together, and now for their presence and sympathy in his sickness and suffering. The Koch nation would always remember this man with respect as the leader who made them great as a nation of warriors, who had blazed a trail of victory and honour, earning respect for the Koch kingdom from many chiefs, kings, and kingdoms of the region.

The person who would feel the loss most was his brother Nar Narayan, king of the Koch kingdom. For the Koch king, the man known as Chilarai had been the commander-in-chief of his forces and the strongest weapon of the Koch kingdom. As Nar Narayan watched his brother, who was suffering and in pain, now only a pale shadow of his former self, he felt a great emptiness, as if Chilarai were already gone. Nar Narayan knew that once Chilarai passed away, it would never be the same again for him and also for the Koch kingdom.

In the next few days, Chilarai's condition deteriorated, and at this time, when his condition was utterly miserable and life was a painful, disease-ridden existence, Chilarai wanted to escape to another world, where he would be free from the misery. He remembered his training in the ashram of Sage Brahmananda and made an effort to make a mental journey to another world in another dimension of his mind. He squatted on a mat on the floor of the shed, facing the river Ganga, and made himself as comfortable as was possible under the circumstances, and then he gradually regulated his breathing and emptied his mind of all distractions and all kinds of pain. It happened slowly, but in time he reached the still, calm, and quiet state of mind, where the pain of his body no longer registered in his mind. He seemed to be in a limbo, waiting for someone or for something to happen, but nothing happened for some time, and he was left waiting a little longer for the unknown. Then suddenly a bright blinding light flashed, and he heard a clear strong voice saying that it was time for the eagle to fly. He suddenly heard the roar of the wind and felt the rush of air sweeping through the small tight hairs and skin that covered his head, and then his eyesight cleared, revealing the world below him. Once again he had become the eagle that was sweeping across the sky. In the distance, the eagle sighted the dense forests covering the foothills of the Himalayas, cascading cataracts, and clear rivers which flowed down from the hills, through dense green forests, and the eagle anticipated the joy of hunting in those regions. In the background it could see the snow-capped mountains and sheer cliffs that dropped from the higher mountains to the deep valleys below. The eagle gave a shrill cry of joy and soared up towards the distant Kanchenjunga Mountain.

On the banks of the river Ganga, someone loudly announced that Chilarai's soul had departed from his scarred and festering body, and on hearing this information, there was a loud and prolonged wailing from the gathered crowd of friends and relatives. His body was cremated at the same site on the banks of the Ganga River, and all his clothes and other meagre belongings in the shed were also consigned to the flames. As a part of the funeral ceremony and to honour Chilarai, a traditional Koch dance to honour the dead was performed by a group of young men and women dressed in their traditional attire. Each participant carried a sword and a small round shield. Male dancers and female dancers stood in alternating positions, forming a semicircle, and at the beginning of the performance they bent down and crouched low on the ground, holding sword and shield together, and gradually rose up in slow motion, rotating the body from the waist up in a circular motion, rising from the crouching position till they were standing upright, and at the same time, they stretched out both hands, holding the sword in one hand and the shield in the other. The hands were held wide apart, and the whole group of dancers moved in a swaying motion. Initially the whole series of movements was done very slowly to the accompaniment of slow drumbeats, and as the tempo of the drum beats became gradually faster and reached a crescendo, the pace and vigour of the dance also became more rapid. This was a dance performed by the Koch during funeral ceremonies for important people belonging to their community. As the dance came to an end and the drum beats stopped, suddenly a shrill cry was heard, *eeeiw–kik–kik–kik–kirrr*, coming from somewhere above. All the dancers and other people who were present looked up in surprise to see that it was a large black eagle soaring in the sky and circling over them on high which had let out the shrill cry. Someone from among the gathered people cried out, 'Chilarai! He has appreciated the performance.' There was a superstitious murmur, followed by a long hushed silence as all who were present at the site continued to gaze at the eagle in the sky. The eagle continued to circle over them for some time even as it rose higher and higher on the rising winds, then slowly it flew away and went out of sight. It marked the end of the Eagle King, and the roll of war drums of the Koch nation became silent forever.

GLOSSARY

Ahoms – the descendants of ethnic Tai people that accompanied the Tai prince Sukaphaa into Brahmaputra Valley in1228 CE and established a kingdom.

Ashram – a hermitage or monastery which serves as a centre for Indian cultural activity, such as yoga, music study, religious instruction.

Bakhtiyar Khalji – a military general of Qutb-ud-din Aibak who conquered Bengal and started Muslim rule in the region. His full name was Ikhtiyar-ud-din Muhammad ibn Bakhtiyar Khalji.

Bamun – another expression for Brahman.

Benares – one of the oldest living cities in the world, also known as Varanasi, located on the banks of the Ganga in Uttar Pradesh and prominent in Hindu mythology.

Bhogi – refers to someone who has volunteered to die in a human sacrifice, a practice that was known in India in ancient times.

Bhuyan – a landlord, a class of rulers in early medieval period.

Bisu – a leader of the Koch tribe, later known as Biswajit Singha.

Black eagle – Ictinaetus malayensis, a large black eagle found in evergreen and moist deciduous hill forests ranging from the western Himalayas to Arunachal and North East Hill states.

Brahmakunda – a sacred water pool which is believed to have miraculous curative properties.

Brahmananda – a learned sage of Benares.

Brahmans – highest ranking of the four social classes in Hindu community, priestly class.

Chaopha – 'heavenly ruler' in Ahom.

Charpoy – a bed with wooden frame and strung with strong strings or ropes, commonly used in India.

Daboia – Daboia Rusellii, Russel's viper, one of the most venomous snakes in India.

Dao – a single-edged broad-bladed sword.

Dashashwamedh Ghat – the main ghat in Varanasi on the banks of Ganga. According to legend, Lord Brahma created the ghat to welcome Lord Shiva and sacrificed ten horses there.

Dikhow- river in Assam which flows near Sibsagar Town.

Dimarua – a territory to the south-east of present-day Guwahati City, comprising a diverse ecological system of hills, valleys, forest, and grassland inhabited by various communities, like Karbi, Tiwa, Garo, Boro, Khasi, Rabha, and others.

Dimasa Kachari – one of the ancient tribes of North East India. They are mainly habitants of present-day North Cachar Hills (Dima Hasao) district of Assam, also found in other parts of Assam.

Driglam namzha – code governing official behaviour and dress in the kingdom of Bhutan.

Ekasarana dharma – neo-Vaishnavite movement established by Sankardev.

Gamocha – a rectangular piece of cloth, usually made of cotton, with red borders on three sides and red woven motifs on the fourth. It is used for various purposes and symbolizes the life and culture of Assam.

Garhgaon – capital of the Ahom kingdom for many years. It was built by Suklengmung in 1540 CE.

Gauda – a historical country or region in ancient eastern India coinciding roughly with present-day West Bengal, Bihar, and parts of Bangladesh.

Gaur – capital city of the Sena dynasty, Pala dynasty, and others in Gauda during ancient times.

Gho – a heavy knee-length robe tied with a belt at the waist worn by men in Bhutan.

Gomatha – a title used by certain bhuyans.

Hemaprabha – wife of Koch leader Bisu and mother of Malladev.

Jayantia Kingdom – formerly a kingdom in present-day North East India that was ruled by Synteng or Pnar tribe.

Kamakhya – a most-renowned Shakti temple dedicated to Kamakhya, the goddess of desire, and located on Nilachal Hill in the western part of Guwahati City.

Kamatapur – capital of ancient kingdom of Kamatapur, which had extended over a large area covering western parts of Kamarupa and north-eastern part of Bengal. Ruins of this city are in Cooch Behar District of West Bengal.

Kanchenjunga – third-highest mountain in the world, rising to a height of 8,586 meters in the eastern Himalayas.

Kangla – ancient capital of Manipur and seat of royal power, located in the middle of present-day Imphal City.

Kangleipak – ancient name of Manipur.

Kareng Ghar – Ahom royal palace in Garhgaon.

Karji – position of minister created by Bisu for the tribal chiefs who helped him.

Kashi Vishwanath Temple – one of the most famous Hindu temples dedicated to Lord Shiva and located in Varanasi.

Khyriem – a territory in the hills bordering Jayantia kingdom in its western side, which was ruled by the most prominent Khasi chief of those times.

Koch – ancient community found in West Bengal, Assam, Meghalaya, Arunachal, Bangladesh.

Kochbehar – a town located in present-day Cooch Behar District of West Bengal, which during the sixteenth century was the capital of the Koch kingdom.

Kshatriyas – one of the four social orders in Hindu society, the rulers and military elite.

Madhabdeb – most prominent disciple of Sankardev, who became his religious as well as artistic successor.

Majuli – large river island in the Brahmaputra, Assam.

Malda – a district in West Bengal famous for mango, jute, and silk.

Malladev – elder son of Bisu who became ruler of the Koch kingdom and was known as Nar Narayan.

Manikya – the title assumed by kings of Tripura. The Manikya dynasty was founded by Ratna Fa in 1280 CE.

Meetei – majority ethnic community in Manipur Valley, belonging to Indo-Mongoloid family.

Meji – the structure made of hay on Uruka and which is set on fire in the next morning.

Mohurs – gold coins.

Morang – a place in southern Terai, or plains of eastern Nepal, where a Limbu king established the kingdom of Morang in ancient times.

Mukundadeva – a king of Odisha during the sixteenth century.

Narayanpur – a small town in Lakhimpur District of Assam, where a Koch garrison was stationed during the days of Koch king Nar Narayan.

Nilachal Hill – a hill on the western part of Guwahati City in Assam, on which the famous Kamakhya Temple is located.

Nyishi – one of the largest tribes in present-day Arunachal Pradesh, a hilly state in North East India, straddling over a portion of the eastern Himalayas.

Pachisi – a cross-and-circle board game which originated in ancient India.

Paik – adult male worker who has to render specific service to the state.

Pala dynasty – a Buddhist imperial power that ruled during the eighth to twelfth centuries over an area covering present-day eastern India and most parts of Bangladesh.

Palas – dominant Buddhist imperial power based in Gauda, present-day Bihar–Bengal area, during the eigth to twelfth centuries CE.

Parsuram – one of the seven immortals in Hindu mythology who did terrible penance under Lord Shiva, was taught martial arts and presented with an indestructible axe-shaped weapon.

Pitha – a type of Assamese pancake with fillings of sesame seeds or coconut, made on special occasions and festivities.

Pranam – a form of respectful salutation.

Sakta – a worshipper of the mother goddess, consort of Shiva.

Sankardev – a figure of religious and cultural importance in fifteenth to sixteenth century Assam who was a saint-scholar, poet, playwright, and socio-religious reformer.

Sattra – monasteries which were used to propagate neo-Vaishnavism in fifteenth-century Assam.

Sena dynasty – a Hindu dynasty that ruled Bengal in the eleventh and twelfth centuries.

Shravan – fifth month in the Hindu calendar, coinciding with late July to third part of August.

Simul – Bombax ceiba, a silk cotton tree which grows mostly in tropical and subtropical areas of the Indian subcontinent.

Solang ghar – audience hall in the Ahom royal palace.

Subansiri – one of the largest tributaries of Brahmaputra River, originating in Tibet region, flowing through Arunachal to join the Brahmaputra near Majuli.

Sukhampha- son and successor of Ahom king Suklenmung. He ruled from 1553 to 1603. During his rule, the Ahom soldiers lost in the battles against the Koch led by Chilarai.

Sukhlengmung – fifteenth Ahom king, who established the capital of the Ahom kingdom at Garhgaon.

Sukladhvaj - second son of Bisu, later became famous by the name Chilarai, meaning 'eagle king'.

Surma River – a major river in Bangladesh which originates as Barak River in India.

Sylhet – a major city on the banks of the Surma River in north-east Bangladesh.

Tezu – a town in Arunachal Pradesh and headquarters of Lohit District.

Twipra – a large historical kingdom of the Tipra people in North East India.

Uruka – the night on the eve of Magh Bihu Festival when young men go to the paddy field and construct a makeshift cottage with hay and bamboo and spend the entire night singing Bihu songs, playing games, and feasting.

REFERENCES

1. Wikipedia, the free Encyclopedia.
2. *A History of Assam* by Edward Albert Gait.
3. *A Comprehensive History of Assam* by S. L. Baruah.
4. *Ahom Buranji- From the earliest time to the end of Ahom Rule*, transalated and edited by Rai Sahib Golap Chandra. Barua.

Printed in the United States
By Bookmasters